Dimension Travel VI: The Ending

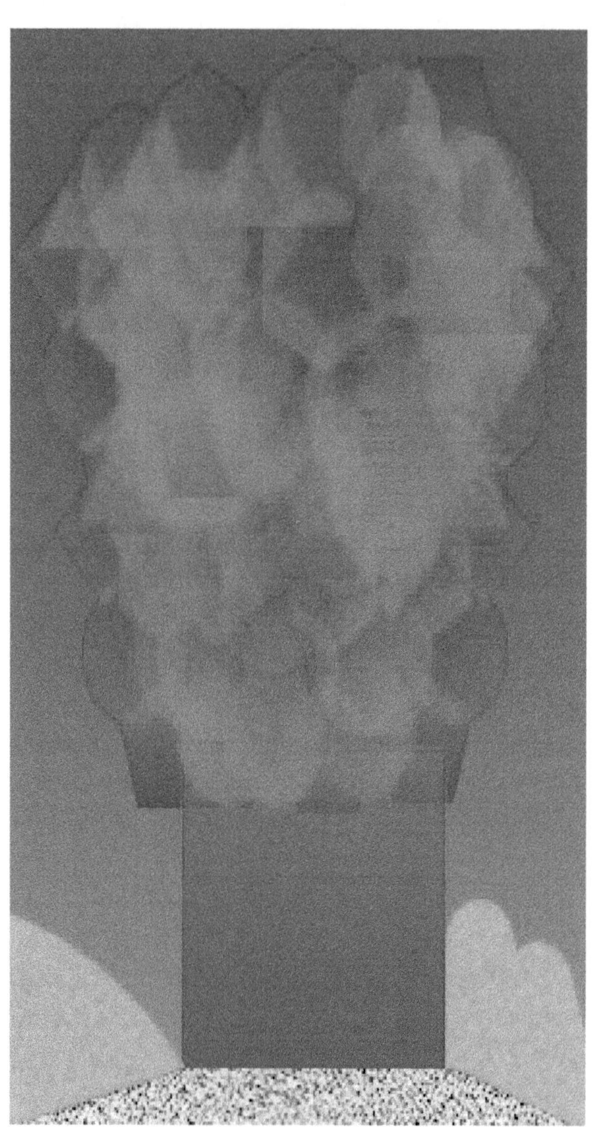

Dimension Travel VI:
The Ending

To:

God, for giving me the talent and creativity to write this book; to my mother, Lisa Esposito, for being supportive of me in writing this book; to my family, for being there for me when writing this book; and to you, the reader.

Copyrighted Material

Copyright control number: TXu002020024

ISBN number: 978-0-9968889-4-3

Contents

Prologue:

Freedom is a treasured gift that very few can declare to have to the fullest extent. Freedom was never handed to anyone on a silver platter. Instead, it was fought for with sacrifice and heroism. When freedom has been obtained, it must be kept protected. Thus, there will have to be a continuous fight for freedom. Although freedom always wins, there will always be insurgents and those, who will try to steal it by conquering lands or attempting to conquer lands. However, they will lose, even if they have thought they have one. Freedom is a treasure that one must never sacrifice; but there has to be sacrifices for freedom sometimes.

Chapter I: New Year's Day: State of the Union Address

It is now afternoon in Starmos City, the alien leader has been in office for about two months as being the office holder for President of Starmos City. Today, he will be the one who will be swearing in every single member of the Parliament. There are four members who represent different districts in Starmos City. The Parliament in the alien city is similar to the House of Representatives in the United States. There are four parliamentary districts in Starmos City. Three of the parliamentary districts are governed by members of the Starmos Independence Party, a Centrist, Populist Party. The minority in the Parliament is the Conservative Party. This party believes in a theocratic republic. Although the majority of the citizens were once forced atheists, now 99.9% of the citizens of Starmos city are Christians: either Catholics or Protestants.

The Alien Estate has the, once called the Royal Hall for the reign of tyranny, now the Parliament Hall. Located at the far left part of the hall, is the seats dedicated for the representatives. In the middle, there are seats meant for the usage for the senators in Starmos City. There are three vacant spots established for the future zones in Starmos City. This bicameral legislature will expand as the city becomes larger. Starmos City was once an At-Large area where Cornelius Von Alien ruled the city. There was not any component of representation for the citizens of Starmos City. Now, at least there is some form of representation. The Parliament has to be fully established with filling up more seats; but, as the city grows, the number of seats will increase.

At each seat right now, there are desks where the representatives have a Bible and typewriter. In the present day, there are few representatives. It is approximately eleven in the morning. The alien leader finished the breakfast that was prepared for him by his wonderful wife, Rubi. The Vice President is the President of the Parliament. Being that the majority party is the Starmos Independence Party, there will be a Speaker of Parliament Pro-Tempore. The Pro-Tempore Speaker only shows up to work when the Vice-President is not present in Starmos City or when he is not able to be at his job. When he retires from his job, then the Pro-Tempore Speaker succeeds him in the seat. The Starmos Conservative Party has three members in both the Parliament and Senate. The two senators in the two Senatorial Districts are both Conservatives and one Parliament member belongs to the Conservative Party. The Conservative Party is the Minority Party in the Parliament. Thus, there is a minority leader, who handles the issues that take place in the Conservative Party.

Within the past couple of months, there have been candidates pushing to create the Remove Von Alien Party, or the Socialist Party, which has been around to reinforce tyranny. This party has been currently under investigation for committing an atrocity to a local business and driving it out of the city. This party is not able to be abolished unless voted out or investigated to the point of justifiable arrest. Being that the tyranny of Starmos City has been gone, Will cannot place somebody under arrest simply because he or she belongs to a party. He can place the indiviual(s) under arrest if they belong to a party committing atrocities in the city. Mr. Von Alien is a fighter for justice in Starmos City. Will is a member of the Starmos Independence Party, which is a party that believes in a free society that fights against tyranny and fights for justice, peace, kindness, chivalry, and honor. The alien leader, brought this city from a troubling city, where tyranny and evilness dominated to a city where justice and peace prospered and where there was a symbiotic relationship between government and the citizens. Present in Parliament Hall, are all four members of the Parliament, Two members of the Senate, the leaders of the lands outside of Starmos City, and the citizens of Starmos City.

There are one hundred citizens who are present in the room because a majority of the citizens, in spite of being proud of the new formation of government, refused to attend because of their time of respite. The meeting is about to begin. All three hundred fifty individuals present in the room are clapping being that the alien leader is entering the room. The song *Hail To The Chief* is being played by the orchestra standing in the rear room behind the Parliament Hall. Will is dressed in typical, political attire. His sartorial appearance makes him have an extremely dapper look. He is wearing a black suitjacket and suit pants. Narrow grey stripes run down this attire. The alien leader is pleased to see his constituents and they are reciprocating that same appeasement for the alien leader walking in the room. He walked up to the Speaker of the Senate, Vice President Brutis, Pro-Tempore Speaker, majority leader, minority leader, majority whip, and minority whip. He walked up to the citizens in the front row, greeted the male citizes with a high five, greeted the female citizens with a small kiss, and welcomed the members of his administration with a formal handshake.

He has now arrived at the podium. Every individual who is present in the Parliament are all applauding the alien leader's arrival. The Speaker of the Senate, Vice President Brutis, is administering the oath to all of the members of the Parliament. First, the Parliamentary Representatives. Rep. Brown, the member of the Independence Party was inaugurated. Followed by that, Rep. Foster, the member of the Conservative Party. Then, Rep. Guynor, the member of the Independence Party. And Rep. D'Moniyhan, also a member of the Starmos Independence Party. Every single representative, stated these words.

"*I solemnly swear to support the Constitution of the United States, the Constitution of Starmos City, and that I will faithfully execute the laws of the land with honor, pride, dignity, and chivalry. I swear to serve my constituents for the needs of their community and I will work with others to reform and improve the community, for which I serve.*"

After those oaths were administered and upheld, the citizens and dignitaries in the room applauded. Followed by that, the senators were brought in. Being that there are currently two Senatorial Districts in Starmos City, both Conservative, minority party members were sworn in.

Senator Worschinskwitz, Rubi's distant cousin and Senator Livingstone. Senator Worschinskiwitz was born in Russia and emigrated to Starmos City over the course of the past couple of years to help Rubi with her job. She ran in the Senate Elections, which took place on December 27, 2047. Senator Livingstone was born in California County and he is Officer Johnstone's half-brother. Brutis administered the oath both the lady and the gentlemen into the Senate.

"I solemnly swear to support the Constitution of the United States, the Constitution of Starmos City, and that I will faithfully serve all the citizens living in my district. I will also make sure that the issues taking place in their district are being properly addressed. If I refuse deliberately to fulfill my duty, I will garnish my position and wage as Senator."

After the senators made their oaths, everyone started cheering and applauding. Speaker Brutis banged his gavel on the circular pad on his desk. The Parliament Hall became silent.

"Thank you very much for your cooperation. I am extremely proud that Starmos City became the way it is today. Let me share that I was once in your position being forced to serve in the Starmos Socialist Governmental Military, and I realized that it is important that justice comes first for the citizens of Starmos City. So, I fought with Will against the terrible tyranny of Cornelius, and we won. Now, I am here as your vice president and the President of the Parliament. I would like to thank every single one of you for participating in this event. I want to thank the public service individuals, who are working hard to fight for we, the citizens of Starmos City, whether it is us being the natural born aliens or the foreign individuals. It is my honor and pleasure to work with you today and to bring a great friend of mine, Will Von Alien to the podium. He is a terrific leader. He definitely deserves all the clapping. He was the one that brought this city to the way it is today. And the least we can do is thank him through applause."

A massive wave of applause starting running through the individuals present in the Parliament. Cheers started sounding the loudest it has ever been. Everyone started lauding the alien leader and singing honorable praises to him. *Battle Hymn Of The Republic* is being sung in the crowd. The alien leader walked up to the podium. After five minutes of this high adulation, the crowd simmered.

"Thank you so much. I do not deserve this. Every single one of you all deserve this. You were the ones that brought this city to the way it is today. Tell Brutis to stop filling up my head." He laughed. "Now, everyone, you were the ones that brought this city to the futuristically thriving city. I want to say that this journey that I have been on board with you has been a long one; but, it was one worth taking. In general, one cannot take the easy road to getting to the place where he or she wants to arrive at. The easy road is not the answer. We must take chances, we must fight if we must fight, we must be tenacious in our work. If we were to take the easy way out, we would not have been where we are today. We would have been still living under the tyranny of that brute, Cornelius Von Alien. I cringe when I mention that beast's name. The best part was that he was my cousin. It is crazy that I call my cousin a tyrant. I have a personal story that I would like to share; but, it is way too sad for me to share. I want to make this clear though. We did not get our freedom on a silver platter. It was not a cake walk to get our rights. In fact, it was a lengthy challenge. It was a fight where one's heart would skip a beat every time he or she made a move in this crusade for justice. However, we did it and we got it done. I would like to thank God for this wonderful action because without God, we would not be where we are today. When we thought that Starmos City was going to be free after Cornelius was killed, it wasn't free. That was because of his former fiancée, Jacqueline Langyaw. We had a second battle to fight when she led a cold-blooded militia of tyrants. We thought that freedom would last for such little time when she and her tyrants tried to take over but, her reign was short lived. We destroyed her band of tyrants and made sure that they received justice, and that was the death penalty. We thought that battle was over. When I was inaugurated, when the dignitaries and I were in the parlor room, a bloody scene took place, where two burglars who were acting as spies for Jacqueline shot a leader of a great sovereign nation, who helped us in the First War Against Tyranny. We had to bring them to justice and I was placed in a camp in the Land of Noma. I prevailed and justice prevailed, at the end of the day. They were punished and sentenced to death for taking the lives of innocent individuals. This was not done because of me. It was done because of you. You were the ones who motivated me to take the actions that I have taken. You were the ones who helped me with this. You were the ones who had the morale to support justice. You were the ones who had the power to bring kindness and peace. You will be the ones who expand this city. We must as a city rise up from the battles that we've encountered. And we will not let our guard down for one second because sadly, there's always somebody trying to be a detriment to freedom."

Everyone in the Parliament Hall started applauding. The members of Will's administration started crying tears of joy. Everyone was cheering. He gulped his drink and sat down. He spoke with the Speaker of the Parliament.

"Why is everybody sitting down?" he asked.

"Will, I don't think you realized, but you became...how can I put this..an idol. You know how idols act. Those who follow idols act like parrots. They do whatever the idol tells them to do, speaks the way the idol speaks, quotes the idol on a consistent basis, and the idol dominates their daily lives. Although you definitely deserve some adulation, I think you should be aware that you are the president of this city and idolatry should not be your philosophy. Your philosophy as leader is the belief where you serve the citizens", said the vice president.

"I am can concur and understand with what you are saying. You brought up a very good point. I will not act like somebody's idol or king because we fought a revolution against a tyrant, who thought himself to be an idol and who had a massive ego. I should not give into my weakness. I shall act with rationale as the leader, certainly not act quixotic. I will ensure that Starmos City always remains in the hands of the governed. The citizens of Starmos City deserve me as the leader. I am going to return back up to the podium in one second to continue the speech", replied the alien leader.

Will returned back to the podium to continue his speech. Everybody stood up from their seats and started praising him, once again. He returned to the microphone.

"Thank you all for being so kind in letting me take a quick break. I already mentioned what has happened. Now, I am going to mention to you about the goals for my administration as president. My job as your president is to handle many fundamental issues. The first issue is to handle public order. In spite of having freedom, your freedom is not unlimited. The reason why is because the society will not be civilized if that is the case. I am not saying that we are returning back to a tyrannical government; but, I am not saying that this city will be a free-for-all and foo-foo-ras will not take place here. We must maintain an important and fundamental factor called public order and safety. We have changed Starmos Common Law to make sure that the citizens are treated fairly, both the law-abiding citizens and the law-breakers. Hopefully, in this crowd, there is not a single law breaker. Hopefully, I have a well-behaved crowd. I am sure that is the case because you all are acting respectful. Instead of establishing prisons for offenders, I will establish Work Farms. You can live your lives at your residence with an ankle bracelet; but you are to show up to work and build the structures for absolutely no pay. That is if you are convicted of a crime. My envision of a justice society is to make sure that there is not a single prison being built. The only prison that is to be built is the death row. I will address that next in my speech. An individual convicted of a felony will have to work on the Work Farms because he or she will learn the lesson of work and establish a better life when that individual gets released from the farm. The big reason why I want to establish the Work Farms is so that way infastructure is built along with productivity for the citizens. Not only that, but also, I want to make sure crime does not increase. Although Cornelius was a strong supporter for this punishment, he supported it for the wrong reason and that was to persecute his dissidents and to eradicate the fighters for justice. I support this kind of punishment because it brings justice for the victims. Although a provision was set on this to have it abolished for a temporary amount of time, I am going to sign and enforce it for the following crimes. Before I get into that, I am going to tell you what this kind of punishment is known as, it is known as the Death Penalty. I am going to enforce the Ray Gun Squad. In order to receive the Death Penalty in this city under my administration and future administrations, the jury will have to vote on the sentence, not the judge, and certainly not the leader. The Death Penalty will be applied for those who commit crimes against humanity, genocide, war crimes, capital murder, and abduction. We are going to sign this into enforcement because it is justifiable. I hope that every single one of you would support my belief on the Death Penalty because it is justifiable in some cases. If you all remember the names I mentioned earlier, they were sentenced to death by a jury of their peers, and the crimes they committed were atrocities against, we, the citizens. At the same time, I will make sure the accused have certain rights. When taken in booking, the fugitive will be able to make the plea to not testify or divulge any information about the crime. Furthermore, I would make sure, that the fugitive has the right to a fair, open, and speedy trial where the attorneys have the right to speak and prepare accordingly in the trial. Also, I would make sure that in Capital Punishment cases, I would ensure that there are a large number of appeals set for the defendant, and I would make sure there'd be at least two investigations in the case: a preliminary trial investigation and a post-sentencing investigation. This is so that way not a single innocent individual ends up being wrongly prosecuted and wrongly sentenced. Like the victims having rights, the accused is able to have rights. One thing that is for certain is that there must be order maintained in the public because there will be chaos. We will turn into a 451 World if that is the case. If there is neither any balance nor order, then there won't be any justice. And without justice, we will return back to the old days. And when we go back to the old days, that means that our society has failed, and a failed society is not what we want. We want a successful society, and maintaining public order is one of the key components to maintaining a successful society. The second issue that I must address is the fiscal issue. We, unfortunately, do not have any debt to owe to any country, nation, or land. We are safe. However, we have to start building revenue for this city. As I said at my inauguration speech, we are going to connect this city to the outside World. Later, this week, I am going to have a ground-breaking ceremony for the establishment of a super highway leading outside of the city and leading to the future airport. We want all forms of transportation coming here. All we have is five roads. We are not considered to be metropolitan or even contemporary. Our city is behind on that. My job is to break through the hills of this city and establish more structures. We will get that done. We will build this city like they did with the Land Of Noma. Although I was stuffed on a train and sent to an arbitrary hidden camp, I was given a tour of the land after I was released, when I found the city to be beautiful. Why can't we make our city like the Land of Noma? Another issue that I have within our own city is urban development. My goal is to bring at least forty hotels for the city to bring competition in the hotel industry, establish zones for shopping and entertainment, and not allow too much red tape on the businesses. We will make sure that you can freely establish and manage your business in this city. This city deserves this. I am going to establish more city parks. This is so that way everybody in the city can enjoy a nice day with the family and make sure it is high quality. With your help, we will be able to turn Starmos City from a city that looked unattractive because of a tyrant to a beautiful city, where everybody can live comfortably. The government and the citizens will work together. The government will not treat any of you like you are immature individuals. Rather, we will treat every single one of you like you are adults. It is important that you are able to participate freely in the government. Problem #1 is handled. Now, we will handle the second problem. Problems must be addressed and solved. That is our job. This address is here to not only highlight our achievements, but also, to discuss our problems. I want to thank you very much for listening to this part. We will handle part three of this speech in a little while. For now, you all can mingle and get some Hors D'Ouerves. Thank you very much for listening. God Bless every single one of you", said Will.

The waiters and waitresses entered the different refreshments and delicacies. There are approximately ten waiters and ten waitresses in the room, twenty in total. Five of whom are establishing the buffet tables for the Hors D'ouevres. All of the servers entered the room dressed in perfect uniform and walking in a sharp manner similar to that of a soldier.

The men are dressed in white pants and a navy blue shirt. There are gold buttons that are found across the top of the shirt. The females are dressed in velvet skirts and crimson shirts. The females have flat caps. The first two men have bald heads and brown mustaches. Their eyes are almond. Their skins are orange color. Followed by that, two blue skin females walked into the room, whose hair colors are blonde. They have hazel eyes. Behind them, two men walked into the room who are fair skin, have dark blonde hair, and blue eyes.

Before them, are two females that have black hair. Their skins are grey color. They are wearing eyeliner. Preceding them, are two males, who have blue skin with three indigo stripes running across both sides of their faces. They have green hair that is cut in the form of a flat top. Before them, there are two females who have red hair, teal colored skins, and blue stripes. After them, there are four males who have brown hair, light green skin, and brown eyes. The first five people started to establish the setting. There is a table on each side of the room. On the right side, this table is serving vegetarian delicacies: Sushi, different assortments of vegetables, different assortments of fruits, and different groups of chips at the table. In addition, there are different groups of chips and breads. There are few carbohydrates at this table. On the other side of the room, there are different meats.

The different meats are at different sections of the table. By the fountain, there's the Sushi Bar. The different Sushis served in this area are California Rolls, Tempura Rolls, Avocado Rolls, Tuna Rolls, and Cucumber Rolls. Right now, one of the servers is slicing the sushi rolls and preparing them for the guests retrieval. Adjacent to this area, there is the meat stand serving differently sliced pieces of meat: Salami, Pepperoni, and different types of meat are served on this particular side of the table. Adjacent to the meat table, is a Lobster Pot. The waiter is butchering the Lobsters, making sure they are edible for the guests.

Adjacent to the Lobster Pot, there's another waiter slicing up the fish meats. The fish meats include Salmon, Tuna, Mahi Mahi, and Flounder. The Mahi Mahi, Tuna, and Flounder were already pre-butchered and cooked for being made edible for the guests' safety. On every buffet table, there are three stacks of one hundred dishes, in case any other guests wanted to come into the event aside from those who are presently at the event. Everyone present in the room is waiting to see Will get his dish first. They are being polite to him. Everybody is staring at him.

"What are you staring at me for and what is your point in doing that?" he asked over the microphone.

The Conservative Parliamentary member answered, "Because we are waiting for you out of a sign of respect. We are honoring you and you deserve this respect."

"That's very nice of you; but if every single one of you all wanted to show respect for me, then you would try and make sure that you would serve yourselves before waiting for me to serve myself. Without you, this government would not work for the democracy that we want, even for something as simple as receiving food before me. That is a sign of respect, in my eyes", the alien leader replied.

Every man and woman in the crowd started lining to get his or her food. After fifteen minutes of receiving food, the members of the Parliament and the guests retrieved their food. The alien leader walked up to retrieve the food. He received about twelve pieces of Sushi, four pieces of Salmon, and some assorted vegetables.

The alien leader finished his task of receiving the food. Along with their Hors D'Oueveres, everyone received different drinks. Every individual is eating at his or her own table in a comfortable manner. The alien leader is sitting on his throne eating his meal comfortably. After fifteen minutes of eating and conversing, the third part of the Starmos State Of The Union Address continued. This time, Will brought a glass of water to the podium, ready to give his oral speech.

"I hope every single one of you are enjoying your dishes. Now, we need to continue with this State Of The Union Speech. In a World, in a country, in a city, in a county, on a street, in a household, and in this city, we need to make sure that there is one thing guaranteed, a basic right. This right is called freedom. If you notice, when I was sworn in, the senate, and the Parliament, we vowed to model our beliefs after the Constitution of the United States. That's because the U.S. Constitution ensures protection and guaranteed rights for the citizens. We are going to do the same here. We are going to encourage different places of worship to come out of the woodwork and build. We will encourage newspapers and different media sources to come out of the shadows and tell the truth. At the same time, we will make sure yellow journalism is not taking place and we are making sure the media does not act defamatory or derisive in its movements. We will make sure the media and the disgusting Court of Public

Opinion does not influence us. At the same time, there is such thing as Freedom of Speech. When Cornelius ruled this city, somebody was not able to challenge his leadership. If somebody disdained his leadership, he would eradicate that individual for good and show absolutely not any mercy. This is not going to be the case in the 'new' Starmos City. The case in the new Starmos City is the citizens will have a right to voice their own opinion with regards to the government. The citizens can disdain my leadership, although there should not be any reason why my leadership of bringing this city to freedom, should be disdained. Now, if one attempts to assassinate me, that's a crime. Freedom does not mean a free-for-all. Yes, freedom is a natural-born right. Yes, freedom is a prerogative; but infringing on my freedom of breathing or anybody else’s freedom of breathing in this city or any other place is not tolerated and the individual involved will be held accountable for that kind of a crime to the greatest extent of the law. Another freedom that we will discuss is the Freedom to Petition and Assembly. I removed the fencing around the Alien Estate so I can hear you, so I can understand your problems, so I can be with you, and so I can make clear and express this estate not only belongs to me, but also to you. The citizens of Starmos City deserve the right to petition. If they want to bring a law to the Parliament, then they are able to bring the law right to the Parliament unobstructed. If they have an issue with a decision that was taking place in this house, they are entitled to complain or freely express their grievances. They are not allowed to break the windows and destroy the value of this estate. The third freedom that I want to make clear is that you will be able to have Freedom of Movement. I am not like Cornelius who mounted guards at the borders of Starmos City. If you want to leave in a legitimate manner or an illegitimate manner, then that is your prerogative. If you leave here legitimately, most likely, you will be welcomed to visit. If you leave here in an illegitimate manner, then it will be extremely hard for you to come back because there will be some severe interrogation. I will not be a tyrant and have the guards shoot you if you leave legitimately. However, I will not be a loose man who just lets anybody come into the city whenever they want. This ties into the idea of public order. When Starmos City turns into an open border place, then there is a de- securing of the borders, which leads to open border anarchy. I can rest assure you that for the citizens who have been living here or who have been born here won't have to suffer through paying the punishment by being denied freedom of movement because of open border anarchy. I will pass a law in the Starmos Constitution that is un-amendable. This law is that not a single alien, person, or individual will be placed into forced servitude unless punished because of a crime that was committed. In this city, I want to say that freedom should always prevail. They say, 'Let freedom ring for all', and what they say is one thousand percent the truth.

You cannot take away freedom; but you can limit it. With freedom, comes limits. Some folks think, the word 'freedom' means you can do whatever you want, whenever you want, however you want, and whoever you want to fulfill your action to. That's not the truth. Freedom is a relative subject. Within the Starmos Constitution, we need to make sure freedom is balanced. We need to make sure there is not freedom to the point of a free-for-all. At the same time, we need to make sure that one con-artist will not claim freedom to cause trouble like take innocent individuals and make them live a hard life. For instance, I hate to bring up this individual's name and action; but, I will remind you of Jacqueline Langyaw. She tried to use freedom to enslave Cornelius's dissidents. This will not take place in this city. We will make sure that folks like Jacqueline get punished because forced servitude shall be considered to be a crime against humanity. Let me also note that I will be fiscally Liberal and at the same time fiscally Conservative. Cornelius not only wanted the citizens pay out-of-control taxes but also, give up most of their salaries. That is not going to be the case in the free Starmos City. There will not be any new taxes. In fact, my goal is to cut taxes by 50%. At the same time, we need to work on public works projects so that way we can expand our roads, promote access to the outside World, promote access by many different forms of transportation, and promote development of buildings. With your help, we will do that. I don't want to say that I am begging from we, the citizens, especially the tax payers. However, one thing that is for certain is that we must get some things done. We must work together. I want to make my closing in this speech. Let me tell you all that you have been great to me. In fact, you all have been too nice to me. Are you kissing up to me?..Good, you aren't doing that. I don't want anybody to kiss up to me because you don't need to do such a thing. Neither, do I want disrespect nor do I want to be treated like a king because I am your friend, I am here to help you, I am here to guide you, I am here to work with you, I am here to serve you in spite of receiving a salary, and I am here to honor you. I am here to show love. We must make clear that we are going to improve this city. Within the next two years in my term, I want to make sure that not my agenda but, the agenda and the best interests of the citizens of Starmos City is fulfilled. While, I am here to serve you and the Parliament is here to serve you, you all have to do your part. I will be a role model in maintaining personal responsibility. At the same time, you all have to maintain personal responsibility. We will make sure that this city remains united and that everyone is nice to eachother. Why don't we learn to love one another and be kind to one another? We can be kind by doing something as small as holding the door for a physically or mentally disadvantaged individual or something as great for volunteering for a charity organization, we must get things done and learn to be kind to one another. A great man once said, 'Ask not what your country can do for you but; what you can do for your country.' We, the citizens must maintain this principle and we will. I want to thank every single one of you for working with me. I will make sure that Parliament does not have any shutdowns in this city. I am going to ensure the members of the governing party and the members of the opposition party learn to work with eachother and settle issues in a peaceful manner. This city is not all about war or belligerent attitudes. As a city, we will maintain peace. This is not contingent on my agenda. Peace is the key role to success. At the same time, war is; but we try to avoid war as much as possible unless the best interests of the security for the Starmos citizens are put in jeopardy. In that case, we shall implement war. I know I have to conclude my speech so, on an important note, I want to state that we've achieved a lot to remove tyranny and expunge it. At the same time, we have a lot to get done and under this administration, things will get done. It is important for the sake of the citizens that their bests interests are fulfilled. I want to thank my administration for working with me. I want to thank Parliament for encouraging, promoting, and actually supporting the rights of the citizens. I want to thank my wife who graciously listened to me on this boring, rhetoric, I meant realistic, speech that I have made. And most of all, I want to thank the citizens of Starmos City for helping the fight for justice", Will concluded.

Chapter II: The "Good" Turnaround:

In the interim, when Will finished his speech at the Alien Estate in the Parliament Hall, a couple street intersections down WVA Boulevard, in the hidden tunnels, Jacqueline's former sister Verminia lives. She is a shapeshifting individual. She was once a co-host for the show *Tough Jackie*.

The under ground tunnels were secret tunnels that have been hidden for years under the tyrannical reign of Cornelius. These tunnels were used to hide refugees and Christians. Some parts of the tunnels were used as shelters to house Christians escaping religious persecution from the tyrant. Then, other parts were used to hold church services. Fortunately, Cornelius never found out about those tunnels. The tunnels are made of stone from a quarry. The tunnels are in the form of different archways. The tunnels have interesting appearances.

There are some parts of the tunnels that are rugged due to wear and tear. Then, there are other parts of the tunnels that look as if they are new. Jacqueline's sister enters the tunnels through a sewage cap. On WVA Boulevard, there's a four feet diameter sewage cap. When the underground churches abandoned its shelters because of Will's emancipation of those churches, some of the evil folks moved in.

In order to enter her dark lair, one must head down a ladder of seven bars. In order to come down those seven bars, one must be extremely careful because that person who heads down these bars will be electrocuted. That's if Verminia turns the eletcrificiation mode on. After heading down the seven bars, one walks into a cave, in order to reach her official residence, one would have to swim in toxic waste water. There are sharks in this water that are mutants.

Finally, one reaches the residence after ten minutes of swimming. Her living room has a mundane television that uses the lemons found in the waste water as a form of energy. Parts of the floor in the living room are made of linoleum. Then, there are the parts of the floor that are made of wood that is splintery. In other parts, one can put himself or herself at risk by mistakingly impaling himself or herself because of the perilous wood. It is recommended for one not to walk on these floors. Hidden underneath the living room floors, is an empty cistern with a cap. There is not a ladder in the cistern. Behind the living room is a kitchen. The kitchen

looks like a place with obsolete items: an ice box, a 1980s microwave oven, and a coal heated stove. There is a large knife holder, which can accommodate up to one hundred knives. There are six drawers in the kitchen. There is a bedroom, which is adjacent to the kitchen. The bedroom features a hammock bed.

There's an inoperable computer, which has a grey screen turned on for twenty four hours on a daily basis. This is used as a sensory deprivation noise for those imprisoned in her secret lair. Verminia is preparing the cistern. The television is speaking.

"Verminia, please report upstairs. Your dissident, Will, is speaking."

She cannot hear the television. Meanwhile, at the Alien Estate, Will is greeting all of his constituents and supporters. Additionally, he is greeting those of Parliament. Slowly, everybody is starting to leave the room. About 20 minutes later, everyone departed from the room including the alien leader, himself. Everybody walked to the dining room for dinner. It is approximately 5 in the evening.

The servers and cleaners have just finished cleaning Parliament Hall. The Waiters are speaking to each other. They are discussing about an evil plan, for which they are about to contrive against the alien leader, his constituents, and the members of parliament and the senate. At the same time, they are speaking in a covert manner. They are trying to cover their tracks making sure any of their discussions do not reach out to the guests and dignitaries at the Alien Estate. They want to keep their plan hidden and limited down to the body of servers. It is now 5 in the evening.

All of the members of Parliament, the dignitaries, and guests departed the room to mingle in the parlor room. The waiters, who have the jet black hair, the Blanco Brothers, are contriving of this attack. Their innocent, angelic appearances disappeared to contriving, premeditating appearances. They are planning to cause an attack on the alien leader and his administration. Their grim appearances are turning off the other servers.

"I think you should show your evil side to the alien leader", the two females said.

Everybody commented on the Blanco Brothers's behavior. The blonde females with hazel eyes walked out of the room in disdain. The other waiters scoffed at the the Blancos. The waiters made different threats. The first waiter, who had a blonde flat top threatened Miles Blanco.

"I will make sure that you are dead before you contrive your convoluted plan. You better not commit such a crime to this wonderful leader. Aside from the fact that he is a great boss, he is the leader of this city and you have a tremendous lack of respect. I want to make clear to you that I will ensure that you will pay", said Wilheim.

The servers bluntly departed from the room.

"I will work as an agent for Will and your plan to kill the alien leader and his wife along with his entire administration shall be foiled. I am tired of my great cousin, Will, having to be the constant target. Somebody, somewhere, at some point in time is planning to assassinate him. That is disrespectable, disdainful, and dangerous. Somebody like that who supports evil like you do, Mr. Blanco, ought to be ashamed of himself. There will be justice and I will ensure that it is done through me. You ought not commit an action like this or even make an effort to commit an action like this. As a citizen of Starmos City and as a loyal friend of Will, I shall and must ensure that your plan is foiled. You do not deserve to be living in this city. Your crimes are punishable", said Wilheim.

Wilheim has a blonde flat top hair style. He has green skin with a two inch wide blue line running down his face. He is a silent supporter of Will. He escaped the Alien Estate when he was first arrested ten years ago. He has been living in hiding until Will sent him to the Alien Estate to work as a server. Wilheim attended the primary and secondary schools with the alien leader. Wilheim has been Will's cousin. However, they did not speak in one decade because of the tyrannical reign of Cornelius. Another reason why they did not speak in one decade was because of the revolution that took place, the silent but lethal revolution against tyranny.

Fortunately, Wilheim returned back to Will, and now, Starmos City will be improved for this reason. The blue line in his face illuminates when there is danger. The anger of Miles and Bill Blanco is increasing. They both feel infuriated because of Will's leadership especially the words he mentioned in the State of the Union Speech, their plan is not being supported, the major opposition for their plan, and the perceived belligerent behavior of Wilheim. Wilheim is a Von Alien.

He is a distant relative of Will. Wilheim is nonchalantly walking up to the stairs in the Parliament Hall. Miles and Bill are both twins, both look the same with the bald heads with sides of jet black hair, the massive mustaches, and the hawk appearing eyes. Although both brothers have an evil personality, Miles is more overt with his evil behavior.

He actually makes effort to be more evil. He thinks that his evil behavior is going to bring more self- satisfaction. Bill is an opposite. He is very devious and dubious in the way he makes his moves and plans with regards to his evil behavior. He will show some form of rationale, where he won't lash out very easily like his quixotic brother. Furthermore, Bill contrives of strategies that are lethal, elusive, and swift. Both brothers have lethal attitudes. Both are conniving in their planning, and both will not stop at anything to commit their crimes. They are wanted for the attempted murder of

Emperor Gairdon, twenty years in retrospect.

"What do you think of attacking him, now?" Bill asked in a quiet manner.

His voice sounds like he whispers when he speaks.

"I think it would be justifiable to do such a thing", shouted Miles.

"Shut up. Do you realize he's in the room?" asked the deceptive brother.

"Yes", answered the overt brother.

"I want to be very careful with how things are planned. Remember, the attempted murder of Gairdon?" asked Bill.

"Yes, I clearly remember that. It was a failure because of you. If you wouldn't have fled the scene and let me shoot a second time, then he would have been dead. Unfortunately, he is still alive. That is disgusting that he's alive. He should be dead, dead, dead! I think it is nothing but a disgrace that he is still alive! How can this be? If you would've kept your mouth shut, he would have been gone and we would not have been in trouble because in Garden City, years ago, when Gairdon first took office, the dungeon was not established. Therefore, we would've been able to get away with it. Nowadays,...", Miles exclaimed.

Wilheim is ignoring the conversation between the two evil brothers that is taking place. He does not even know what they are talking about.

"I would like to have a flashback of how Gairdon was attempted to be killed by us. I need to have some story to increase my adrenaline right now because I want to attack the alien leader", the overt brother said.

He stared into the wall as he made this statement. Both are staring into the wall.

"I remember the day. It was a March 17, 2025. We were stuck in the early 21st century in Garden City. We were living in the mushroom adjacent to the Spazerstocks. We brought our water pressure guns with us. We took our beetle. It ran on wings based on the strength of the never- ending sunshine in Garden City. We brought it down to the Palace. That day, Gairdon was having the Golden Jubilee for his 25th Anniversary as the Emperor of Garden City. I said to you, 'that was the perfect day to kill.' So, I brought the Spazerstocks along with us on the journey. Being that they were spies for Cornelius, they had possession of Ray Guns. They were the ones that pulled the first trigger. They hit a tower on the palace. Then, I took our gun and aimed at the Squire of Gairdon. None of them died. Sadly, I realized I missed. The bullet bounced off one of the Gold Towers left a chip in the tower and then ricocheted in the back of the beetle. Then, I had you shoot Gairdon. That was it", replied the covert brother.

"Comeon, tell me about what I did and how I was involved in the killing. I would strongly appreciate it that you would share that piece of information with me. I want you to bring my part in. Besides, your story was not long enough. Yes, I know it was the truth; but, the your version is not good enough to satisfy me. My adrenaline to kill Will has not increased, yet. Give me some adrenaline. Tell me about what I did. I'd appreciate it if you would encourage me", said Miles.

"Fine, I shall tell you about how you almost killed Gairdon. So, continuing on with the story, you got the gun and cocked the trigger. You shot him. I thought it landed on his head. I saw some bleeding and that might have injured him, which would possibly lead to his death; but, you did hit him, which was a great thing. Unfortunately, he didn't die", replied Bill.

"And what happened next?" asked the overt brother.

"We all fled the scene, but at last we almost succeeded with an assassination of a tyrant. We killed Gairdon, and we are not afraid to kill somebody else, especially somebody like Will. We will let the power of Cornelius prevail. Starmos City needs to have its justice brought back and we shall do it", exclaimed the covert brother.

Wilheim walked over to the closet. He opened the door to retrieve a killer magnet. This magnet would have a field which would destroy one's energy. The magnet looks similar to a musket. The trigger initiates the magnet and the magnet is made of the spear at the end of the musket-like weapon. Wilheim charged the gun making sure it was on green, which would indicate it's fully charged. The alien leader's distant cousin stared at the two conniving and convoluted brothers.

"So, you two are involved in a plan to assassinate Will? Is that correct?" he asked.

"How do you know that?" Miles asked bluntly.

"Because I heard the entire conversation. I was acting like I didn't even know what was taking place in that area where you two were talking, discussing your intricately involved plans to kill the greatest leader in all of the dimensions. I knew that you told a story about Gairdon, and let me tell you something, Gairdon is dead. Being that you two were the first assassins, you two must've had something involved with his death. He died at the Alien Estate because he was killed by Korbian, one of Jacqueline's confidantes. You two should be held responsible for your reprehensible actions. You will be held responsible. I will not stop to go after you. Now, come over here now so, I can fight you", answered the alien leader's distant cousin. "Alright, I will come over here. I am not afraid to destroy you. You might try to harm my plan. However, I will inflict physical harm to the point of demise for you. In fact, I will not inflict harm to the point of death. I will just kill you then and there", replied the overt brother.

He made this statement in an angry manner. His face is turning red in anger. He is sweating. Both brothers are showing signs of disgust and infuriation. Both started running up to Wilheim. The alien leader's cousin is cowering in fear. His bold attitude did not match the intended harm of the evil Blanco Brothers. The brothers are five feet away from the alien leader's cousin.

They stopped right before killing him. Wilheim is staring at the charge of the Magnetic Musket. The charge is only on 20%. It is not fully green and ready to use. The gun is currently locked to the charger.

"I am sorry. Please forgive me, for I have wronged you. I didn't mean to charge this gun. I have to admit that I just wanted to kill you two because you two were ready to attack my cousin and I had to defend my family. I didn't realize that defending my family could bring me a tremendous amount of harm. I am sorry to wrong my favorite cousin, Will, but, I am afraid you would kill me. Spare me my life. I will work as a double agent. I know I am betraying my city but, in order for my life to be spared, I will go as far as committing high treason and facing the risk of being exiled, imprisoned, or possibly executed", the alien leader's cousin said.

"Should we spare his life?" asked Miles.

"Absolutely not, look what harm he's going to bring to us. I don't think we should spare him. He is a danger to our lives. At the same time, I believe that he would be a great double agent. We need a double agent. We will spare his life contingent on that factor alone", answered Bill.

"No, I don't want him to live. Finally, being able to think rationally, I want to say that if he admits to being a double agent, he might tell Will exactly about our plan. While he's working for us, he can text on his Gphone and make a statement to the alien leader. He might add a little hashtag to this and post it to the public on the Gram. Let's kill him. He deserves to die. He has committed crimes of malice against us. For Godsakes, he wants to use a Magnetic Musket, which will cause paralysis to death. I will not spare him his life. I don't care if he wants to plead. He can make all his pleas all he wants. He will still be an imminent threat to our agenda. Do we want that to happen?" asked the overt brother.

"Good point. Let's kill him", the covert brother answered in a nonchalant manner.

They retrieved the gun. The charge of the gun just finished. It is unfortunately too late for the alien leader's cousin to make a move. He grabbed the ankle of Miles.

"Stop! I have something to say", the alien leader's cousin screamed.

"You have ten seconds to explain to me as to why I should not paralyze you or better yet ensure that you are dead", said the over brother.

"I won't act as a double agent. As a matter of fact, we will keep this incident in this room. Not a single man, woman, or deceased soul will find out about this. I don't want to die because I am somebody's son, somebody's cousin, and I love my family. Spare me, for I have wronged you and I am apologetic for my actions. Let me go."

"Okay, I will let you go. This sparing is conditional. You better listen to me. Let me be very clear with you, if you tell anybody about this ordeal, you will perish and go straight to Hell. You will be punished for your actions. So, you better be honest with me and I mean it", said the overt brother.

He made his statement in a harsh way. He grabbed the Magnet Musket and walked out of the room.. Wilheim is lying on the floor still cowering in fear. The two evil brothers walked out of the room, and are walking down the hallway out of the estate. While, the two brothers completed this action, the alien leader's cousin is still lying on the floor.

The door bell rang, which signaled the door was opened. From there, Wilheim screamed. His scream initially sounded inaudible. A second later, he raised the volume in the second scream. He screamed a second time and Rubi heard him as she was walking down the hallway to the alien leader's bedroom to retrieve a gold necklace gift that is worth approximately ten thousand Starmos Bucks.

She heard the scream. A third scream sounded. The volume of the scream is less audible than the first scream. The issue about this scream was that Rubi was alarmed right at the moment when she finished turning the handle to enter the bedroom. She is standing in the middle of the hallway, right in front of the door leading to Parliament Hall.

"Rubi, come over here", shouted Wilheim.

"Who is making such a noise?", the alien leader's wife asked herself.

The alien leader's cousin reiterated his calling verbatim.

"Is this Wilheim?" asked Rubi.

"Yes, it is I, Wilheim Von Alien", answered the alien leader's cousin answered.

"Who are you? I do not have any knowledge of a man named 'Wilheim Von Alien.' I don't know who the hell you are", replied Rubi.

"Well, where are you because I want to get to be able to have more knowledge about you", said the alien leader's cousin.

"Where are you located?" asked the alien leader's wife.

"I am right near the door of Parliament Hall. I am waiting right here lying on the floor and I need help"", said Wilheim.

"Are you making this up? Are you trying to trick me to get me to have knowledge of you?", asked the alien leader's wife.

"Whoever you are, I hope that you do not think that I am a liar. I need to speak with you in a secret room, where not a single individual will be involved in this discussion and that this discussion that I am going to say to you is kept in secrecy and under wraps", answered the alien leader's cousin.

"Okay, I just need to know where you

are located. Specifically, which door I need to enter in order to discuss this issue with you", replied the alien leader's wife.

"No, no, no, no, and no! You are not supposed to discuss the issue right over here, We have to discuss it in a quiet and isolated room. My life is in danger. Somebody is about to kill me", said Wilheim.

"I don't believe you for one second. I am not going to come up to you. You're not worth while to deal with. Do you think for one second that I want to hear your problems?", asked Rubi.

"This is not to be a drama queen or to share a sob story. This is about a threat. I am Will's cousin. You are to let me speak with you", the alien leader's cousin answered.

"I do believe you that you are my husband's cousin. However, there are two things that I want to make clear with you. First of all, you are to have respect for me. I don't want to sound like I am entitled to respect or that I have a massive ego; but, I do want to say that you are not to tell me what to do and I will not tell you what to do or how to do it. Second of all, I want to have some awareness about when the last time you've actually saw Will", the alien leader's wife replied.

"I've been with Will all of his life until ten years ago when I went into hiding. I used to attend primary and secondary school with Will. When his parents died, he was taken to the estate. That was when I last saw him. I went into hiding because I was considered to be an alien, who fought for freedom and justice against the tyranny of Cornelius. I lived in the tunnels underneath the city for ten years. I lived with the churches, at points in my life, because I was a reverend at some churches. If you don't believe me, you can ask my cousin. I don't think it's worth while going all the way back down the hallway to ask Will such a frivolous question. Believe me, every word coming out of my mouth is true. I am respectful to you. I am just scared right now. I would like it if you would take the time to speak with me. Thank you for at least giving me a chance to make a simple statement", said Wilheim.

"Very well, then. We will head to the secret room down in the sub-basement of the estate", replied Rubi. She entered the room and helped the alien leader's cousin stand up from lying on the floor for ten minutes. He stood up. "Where's the door?" he asked. "It's down by the library shelf", the alien leader's wife whispered. They walked down the stairs into Parliament Hall. From there, they approached the back wall. This wall is comprised of a voluminous quantity of books. On the right, near the right stairway, is a bust of Will's head featured on the center shelf. Rubi removed the bust and pressed the red button, which keeps the door open for ten seconds. This is so that way not a single individual, who is not permitted to enter this secret area, does not have an opportunity to enter. The door is slowly opening. Wilheim entered through the library door first. Rubi followed.

"What's down here?" the alien leader's cousin asked.

"I'll tell you in a minute", the alien leader's wife answered.

They are in a small room. Grey pieces of rugged metal are the composition of the wall. There is a television screen emerging from the the ceiling, which is made of concrete. The Head of the Starmos Justice Department, Officer Kerilic is appearing on the screen from police headquarters underneath the estate.

"Who goes here?" he asked.

His eyebrows are crinkled because the video image is not presenting itself in a clear manner. The voice clarity is not concise.

"Who goes here?" he reiterated.

Finally, the voice clarity was tuned.

"It is I, Rubi Worschinskiwitz. I am Will Von Alien, the President, his wife", the alien leader's wife answered.

"What is your purpose of coming in this secret area?" asked the officer.

"I am here because I want to show somebody the secret area because we need to have an important discussion", answered Rubi.

"Who might that individual be?" asked Officer Kerilic.

"His name is Wilheim Von Alien", the alien leader's wife answered.

"I've never heard of a man with the name Wilheim Von Alien. He is not on my list. Do you want me to double check my list in spite of my broad knowledge about this list of names of individuals who are allowed in this area?" the officer asked.

"Yes, I would strongly appreciate it because I would believe his name is on this list. At least, it should be on this list", answered the alien leader's wife.

Officer Kerilic is checking the list of names of who are welcome. Behind the screen, the officer is in front of his desk. The list of names are of the following: Will Von Alien, Light S. Cycle, Rubi Worschinskiwitz, Officer Kerilic, Gairdon, Bill Stone, Tom Jackson, and Joseph S. Pidoriano.

"I am sorry to tell you this but, he is not

allowed in this secret area. One is not allowed to bring any guests in this area because there is some confidential information", replied Officer Kerilic.

"Is there any possible way that my cousin-in-law is allowed down this area? There must be some way", said Rubi.

"Well, I must admit that there is one way. However, it might be lengthy. He would have to go through an interrogation", replied the officer.

"Fine, we'll do it. I don't care how long it takes. It is worthwhile. It's a must that this man must come down here immediately because he needs to discuss something with me in private. I would appreciate it if you do not ask him such a question like that. It's not like we are coming down here to cause trouble, steal anything, or divulge any classified information", the alien leader's wife said.

"Do you care if this interrogation takes up to two hours? Most likely, it will not take that long. It will probably only take twenty minutes. Still, it is important. That is just protocol. I am sure he's a trustworthy fellow; but we must abide by our regulations regarding such an entrance into a secret area", replied Officer Kerilic.

"He can be interrogated. It is important that we serve the best interests of the public first, than those of ourselves. I want to know if there'll be any further processes after the interrogation", said Rubi. "Yes, we will do a scan. Polygraphs are too anachronistic for this time period. We scan folks nowadays. We will scan Wilheim to make sure that he is not a trouble maker or a spy. We will also scan him to make sure he is telling the whole truth and nothing but the truth", replied the officer.

"Very well, then. Would you mind giving me an approximate time of how long this process is going to take from the point of interrogation to the scan?" the alien leader's wife asked.

"The interrogation can take as short as five minutes or as long as one hundred twenty minutes. Then, the scan takes just as long as the interrogation. The shortest time this process will take will be ten minutes. The longest time this process will take is two hundred forty minutes. Like you and I concurred upon earlier, it would be necessary and safer for an interrogation process without taking any chances. I don't believe he is a dangerous risk to divulging any information or committing an act of espionage. However, we do not know. So they say, the devil we know could be living in our house", answered Officer Kerilic.

"Are you trying to insinuate that Wilheim was causing any trouble? Are you trying to insinuate that my cousin-in- law is a danger to this city? Would you think, for one second, I would let this man pass through the library door to come into this secret area? Do you think I would let somebody commit any criminal acts? Would you think I would let danger come into the doors of this estate?" Rubi asked in an angry and defensive manner.

"Absolutely not! I thought we agreed to having an interrogation earlier", answered the officer.

"Yes, but there are some second thoughts about this process. I don't think it would be justifiable for you to investigate Will's cousin, Wilheim", replied the alien leader's wife.

"Too late. There's not any other option. It's either I eject him from the estate or he answers the questions in a proper manner and is scanned after being questioned", said Officer Kerilic.

"Fine", Rubi replied with a sigh of exasperation.

"Okay, sir, can you please give me your name in its entirety?" asked the officer. "Yes, I am Wilheim Von Alien", the alien leader's cousin answered.

"So, you're a Von Alien? Eh? Can you prove it to me?" asked Officer Kerilic.

"I forgot my identification at home. If you do a little bit of research on your computer, you will be able to find me on the Von Alien Family Tree", answered Wilheim.

At the headquarters, the officer retrieved the Von Alien Family Tree. On the top of the family tree is Cornelius and his ex-wife, Nova. Cornelius's name has been crossed out on the family tree. Nova's name has DECEASED written across the top of her face because she died from being sent to the desert when King Haggoth invaded.

Adjacent to her name, are Will's parents. DECEASED has also been written across their names. Wilheim is written below Cornelius's nameless, also DECEASED sister. She died from being shot on the firing squad under Cornelius's tyrannical regime. Officer Kerilic closed the book.

Back at the interview, "Okay, I know exactly who you are. You are Will's cousin. Although that is the case, you would not be able to enter because for all we know, you can still support the tyranny of Cornelius", he said.

"Why are you speaking to me in an accusatory fashion?" the alien leader's cousin asked.

"I am not accusing you of anything. I am just interrogating you to ensure that you are trustworthy. So, continuing on, do you have any criminal history under the leadership or during Will Von Alien's Revolution?" asked the officer.

"I do have a criminal history under Cornelius. I was wanted for committing treason because I was considered to be a fighter for freedom against tyranny. I believed in liberation from the tyrant. Since, that was not Cornelius's core value, he considered me to be a traitor. I was wanted and I lived in secret tunnels underneath the city. Fortunately, when Will became the leader, he exonerated anybody who was a freedom fighter. I was one of the exonerees. I want to make clear that tyranny will not prevail. During Will's Revolution, I was a silent supporter for the freedom fighters. During his presidency, I did not commit any crimes", answered Wilheim.

"You are not in the clear as of yet. I want to know the entire purpose as to why you're coming down here. It is quite important for me to know", said Officer Kerilic.

"Why do you need to know that?" the alien leader's cousin asked.

"Who is the one asking all the questions? Who are you to tell me what questions I am to ask you and what questions I am not allowed to ask you? Who are you to question a single posed question for what I've asked?" the officer asked in a skeptical and angry manner.

"You are the one asking all the questions. You are allowed to tell me to answer any question that you pose. I am to respect those questions and have an answer for those questions and I am to tell the truth. There are no 'and's, if's, or but's' when I ask any question. I am being honest with you", answered Wilheim.

"Good, now you're getting the hint. So, let me reiterate the question I've asked you earlier. What is your purpose of coming down here? Can you please tell me your answer in a cohesive, coherent manner? Will you answer the question in its entirety?" asked Officer Kerilic.

"Yes, sir. Now, I'll tell you what happened earlier for which my purpose of coming down here is. When Will had his State Of The Union Speech, I was working as one of his servers. After the speech, all the other servers and I cleaned up the food mess down in the Parliamentary Hall. The Blanco Brothers: Miles and Bill Blanco were contriving plans to commit an assassination against Will. I heard all about their plan. Initially, I pretended not to hear about the plan. However, my anger was increasing. I was becoming very defensive that my cousin would be the victim of an assassination. Family members protect each other. I did not speak in a belligerent or bellicose manner; but, I did tell those two that I know all about their plans. I was planning to eradicate the

Blanco Brothers will a Magnet Musket. This musket would paralyze the brothers and their paralysis would slowly kill them. Miles ran up to the stairs where I charged the gun. He started assaulting me and he was about to kill me with the gun. I pleaded for mercy a first time. Both brothers refused to accept my plea. Right before I was about to be shot, I pleaded a second time promising that I would not act as a double agent or tell anybody about the altercation in the room. They believed me when the gun was pointed right up to my face. They took the gun and walked out of the Alien Estate. I haven't heard a single trace from them. This only took place about fifteen minutes ago. Basically, I lied to them. As you can see, I am right here right now and I am discussing this issue with you right now. I hope you promise to keep this interview in confidence because if somebody finds out, this whole city will be screwed because these brothers are sociopathic individuals who show little to absolutely no mercy", the alien leader's cousin answered.

"I pity your situation. And I can understand as to why you want to come down here. On the other hand I don't feel that you provided me with enough information about your purpose for coming down here. Can you please be clear with me as to why you need to enter this secret area?" asked Officer Kerilic.

"The reason why I need to come down here is to discuss the situation to Rubi about what happened. Rubi needs to know this information so she can make Will aware of the plan to bolster security around the estate and so that way we can be able to track down the brothers, retrieve the gun, and have them prosecuted in a court of law", answered Wilheim.

"Why can you not discuss this in another area of the estate? Why does it have to be in this area?" asked the officer.

"Because we don't have any knowledge if those conniving, devious brothers are spying on us so that we are also their meat. We don't know that. This is the only area in the estate where things can be kept confidential, and where folks will keep classified information, kept under wraps. We also do not want any of the common folk to take our conversations the wrong way. And we certainly do not want an overzealous prosecutor to accuse us of committing an atrocity against the president", answered the alien leader's cousin.

"That's more than enough information. Protocol does not only tell me to give an interview about the purpose of your visit down in this secret area, but also, to make sure you are aware of Starmos City History. So, I need to ask you some questions that might be considered inconsequential. Do you know what the Starmos Constitution is modeled after?" asked the officer.

"Yes, it is modeled after the United States Constitution, except the rules in our constitution are unamendable without triple permission from Parliament", answered Wilheim.

"Very good. Now, do you know who ran Starmos City for 25 years?" asked Officer Kerilic.

"Yes, I hate to mention this bastard's name; but it was Cornelius Von Alien", answered the alien leader's cousin.

"Yes, him, unfortunately. What kind of government does Starmos City have now?" asked the officer.

"A democratic representative government. It was once a socialist dictatorship", answered Wilheim.

"You answered that one correct. Now, do you know what Starmos City is building within the next five years? Or, name me at least two public works projects?" asked the officer.

"Starmos City is planning on building an airport along with a superhighway. Additionally, they are building a series of residences and businesses outside of the city", answered the alien leader's cousin.

"Brilliant. Do you know how many

Parliamentary and Senatorial Districts there are in Starmos City? Can you tell me about the Majority and Minority Parties in Parliament Hall?" asked Officer Kerilic.

"Absolutely. The majority party is the Starmos Independence Party, the centrist, right-leaning party. The minority party is the Starmos Conservative Party. There are Four Parliamentary Districts. Thus, there are four members who are involved in the Parliament. Three of whom are members of the Independence Party. The Opposition Party in the Parliament is the Conservative Party. There are two Senatorial Districts. Both representatives are members of the Conservative Party. There are more Senatorial Districts to be added when the city expands. To the fullest capacity, the city will have six Senatorial Districts", answered Wilheim.

"Great. Now, I am going to proclaim that you have individual access into the secret area within the Alien Estate. I shall hereby sign your name onto this list. You, Wilheim Von Alien, are to keep the information down here in secrecy unless permitted by the alien leader of his wife. You are welcome into this area. However, I shall now scan you", declared Officer Kerilic.

At the headquarters, he hit the scan button. A blue laser beam is running across Wilheim's body. The scan finished. The word

PROCESSING is shown on the screen. Two minutes later, the officer's face returned back on the screen.

"Welcome to the Secret Lair of the Alien Estate. Please be careful. Welcome. I hope you find out your way back to the estate", he said.

He hit the button to open the double, twenty four inch thick metallic doors into the lair. The alien leader's cousin and Rubi stayed in the room.

"What are you still doing here?" asked Officer Kerilic.

"I am skeptical as to why I am supposedly heading out of the Alien Estate. I thought this lair was located within the estate", said the alien leader's cousin.

"It is technically below the estate. Therefore, it is not in the estate", replied the officer.

"Well, I am sorry that I didn't realize that", said Wilheim.

"You don't have to be a smart ass", replied Officer Kerilic.

"How do you know that I am or not being a smart ass?" asked the alien leader's cousin.

Chapter III: The First Part of the Secret Lair

The alien leader's cousin has just been given access to the Secret Lair in the Alien Estate. He and the officer are fighting and quarreling back and forth regarding a nonsensical issue.

"You are nothing but a smart ass", said the officer.

"How come you are saying such a thing?" asked the alien leader's cousin.

"You are making a big issue out of such a little thing. You have an issue with the Secret Lair being downstairs or not being part of the estate. I don't have any knowledge of the exact reason why that's the case, but whatever your belief about the location is your prerogative and opinion. Personally, I believe your opinion is stupid and idiotic", answered Officer Kerilic.

"How come you think that's the case?" asked Wilheim.

"Because you have an issue with the location of the Secret Lair. I've already let you enter the doors. What else do you want me to do for you? Teleport you there? I don't think so. I don't think you should question anything about this estate. If you question anything regarding the configuration of this estate, especially under your great cousin's administration, then that is a disgrace. I might consider removing you from the list to have access into this lair. You are making a mountain out of a molehill regarding this place, for which I've just given you access to. Are you serious?" asked the officer.

"No, are you serious? You are the one who's making the mountain out of the molehill regarding this lair. You are making an issue about me simply questioning the location of the lair. In this city, I believe it's one's prerogative to question anything. He or she who questions anything can receive an answer without a question. I questioned you about why the area is in the present location. You had an issue with that, which I quite frankly saw as stupid. You think you are this intelligent individual. Meanwhile, you are not. All you do is sit behind a desk, write down names, read questions from a questionnaire sheet, and hit a button, which determines who is allowed in the Secret Lair. Then, you chose to be critical and argue about an issue. How about we both drop this. To be honest with you, I think it would make a lot of sense that we drop this argument because I believe it was quite frivolous", answered the alien leader's cousin.

Officer Kerilic's face on the screen is turning red in anger. In fact, his veins are popping out of his head. His lips are tightening and his eyes are squinting. He is lowering his eyebrows. His hands are tightening into fists. He crossed his hands and placed them below his chin. He made this particular hand motion to prevent his anger from damaging items on his desk.

"Let me tell you something. Who do you think you are to insult my job? I have many more roles to my job than you think. Do you think it's your right to insult my job and ridicule my roles? I don't think so. I can easily ridicule your roles. How would you like it if I said all you know how to do is clean tables and wait tables? I don't think you would like it at all. I not only have an issue with that comment that you made, but I also have an issue with you questioning the reasons why I am continuing to fight you on this. You think that I am trying to continue this fight. However, I am not. I am not the one who is being immature. You are. Wilheim, you need to reassert your behavior. For your idiotic behavior and deprecating remarks, I will hereby refuse to let you enter the doors of the Secret Lair", Officer Kerilic said bluntly and angrily.

The doors are shutting. There's a number above the double doors making a countdown from 30.

"Both of you. Shut the hell up! You men are acting so immature. You, officer, open the damn doors. You, Wilheim, shut up because you are being a nuisance. Both of your behavioral actions and words are pejorative. You two should be ashamed of yourselves. Now, Officer Kerilic, I am telling you to open these doors now. Put a halt to the closing process and open the damn doors. I mean it. So help me, God, your behavior needs to stop", the alien leader's wife said.

"You do not have any right to speak to me in that kind of manner. Are you going against me like Wilheim? Is that what you're doing, yes or no? You better give me a few good reasons as to why I should let you and Wilheim into the chamber. And I mean it. They better be good reasons. I swear", replied the officer.

Both individuals calmed down.

"Fine, I am not going against you or Wilheim. I am just saying that your behavioral actions were very immature. For Godsakes, you two are quarreling back and forth about an issue that is not important. Now, there are two big reasons as to why I would like Wilheim and I to enter this place. Primarily, for him to discuss with me an important issue that must be discussed in secrecy. Secondarily, to show him the Secret Lair being that he's never been down here before. I think those are two very big reasons to reopen the doors", replied the alien leader's wife.

"Oh, yeah, those are very big reasons for me to open the doors. It is so nice of you to tell me that I am being frivolous with the way I am fighting. You two can just come on in. I really wouldn't mind it if you two decided to enter those door", Officer Kerilic said in a sarcastic manner.

"Do you think I am stupid. Do you think I do not know the mannerism for which you are speaking in? Well, you're totally wrong. I know exactly the way you're speaking. You're trying to be condescending to me and you're being nothing but a sarcastic smarty pants. I am not like that. One of the kinds of folks that I despise are sarcastic individuals. Liars are just as bad. Thieves are the ones who I hate the most. Don't get on my bad side. You have already entered Wilheim's bad side. Who is to say that you're not going to get on my bad side? Your behavior is very absurd and it should stop right now. I think you should just let us in. You get my point. Do you not?" asked Rubi.

"I understand your point. At the same time, I am not going to let you and Wilheim in. You've ridiculed me based on my sarcastic comments. Isn't there such a thing as what I'd like to call 'freedom of speech?' I believe there is such a constitutional law. So, I can have you apprehended for violating the Starmos Constitution. If you do that, you're screwed. You're not only committing the crimes against me by denying me the right to freedom of speech. However, you're denying your husband's constituents their rights by violating them. I don't think you want to die. Or, do you? If you violate your constituents' rights, then you will be apprehended and sentenced to death. Besides, isn't that considered to be crimes against humanity?" asked the officer.

"I am not violating your rights. I was one of the folks who helped my husband fight for the rights of the Starmos citizens. And you're telling me that I am taking away those rights. Now, let me tell you something. Just because we have rights, doesn't mean we have a free-for-all. You are not allowed to lie, you are not allowed to steal, and you shouldn't be sarcastic. If you're going to take me to court for constitutional violations and crimes against humanity, then you are acting in an absurd and ridiculous manner. Additionally, you are acting in an arbitrary way. Arbitrary behavior should not be tolerated in this city. Technically, I can bring you up on rights violation charges and then you will not be able to think straight because you're dead. How do you like your own ideology of making up false charges to shut somebody up?" the alien leader's wife asked.

"You are despicable. How can you say such a thing? Are you trying to make a death threat to me? If you are, you will pay the severe price. A death threat is not meant for this place. Your sinister behavior will not be allowed. I would never make any death threat or try to inflict harm to you because I am way too kind unlike yourself. Rubi, you are one of the most arrogant and nasty individuals I know. You should really be ashamed of yourself. Folks like you are not meant to live in this city. Folks like you are not meant to be living in this World. Folks like you are not meant to be living in all of the dimensions. Folks like you are not meant to be living in all the universes. Folks like you are not meant to be living period! Therefore, you will pay the price and that will be death. I will be the one who kills you", answered the officer.

"You are telling me that I made death threats toward you when you were the one who made death threats toward me first. You were the one who wanted to inflict harm against me. There's not any room for anybody like you. You are not meant to be living. You are telling me that Wilheim is not welcome to enter the room. Let me tell you this. I think that such a frivolous fight is not worth while and such a thing turned into death threats and possible inflicted violence. I think there's more to this than what meets the eye. I think you have been the one who has been wanting to kill me all along. You have just been waiting for the perfect moment. I know exactly how your psychotic mind works. You are plain evil", replied the alien leader's wife.

"I am not evil. I was not always evil. I was the one who rescued your husband from possibly dying in the Land Of Noma. I was the one who apprehended the killers of Emperor Gairdon and made sure they received the death sentence. Are you a true wife? Are you somebody that helps your husband in sickness and in health? Are you somebody who fights for justice for your husband? I don't think so because all you know how to do is cry. You try and evade every situation possible. You weren't the one who cared about your husband who you apparently didn't know he was kidnapped and tossed in a cistern. You disregard your husband. I bet you if you found him or somebody that looked like him on the side of the road, you would show little to no regard. You are a mooch and a parasite. I know exactly why you married Will. You married him so you can live at this estate. This was so that you can escape the boxcar that you have been living in out of choice for many years. You are nothing but an elitist gold digger. I bet you for one second if Starmos City went down the tubes, you wouldn't do anything to protect the city. You only care about this estate and that's it. Rubi, don't try and put on an act in front of all the citizens because we all know the real Rubi. The real Rubi is a self-centered, egotistical woman. The real Rubi is somebody who doesn't care about the citizens and their rights. Therefore, I think I should kill the real Rubi", Officer Kerilic stated in an investigative manner.

The alien leader's wife is running to the library door. Wilheim remained in the room. She walked out of the entrance room to the Secret Lair and retrieved the bust from the library door. She returned back into the entrance room to the Secret Lair. The officer is still on the screen.

"What are you going to do with that bust?" he asked.

"I am not going to tell you", the alien leader's wife answered.

"You better tell me or else I am going to kill you right now", said Officer Kerilic.

"Didn't you tell me you were going to kill me earlier?" asked Rubi.

"Yes, I did. However, at that time, I was going to give you the opportunity to make the final plea for mercy. Being that you have that bust, I don't know what you're about to do. So, you better tell me otherwise I am actually going to kill you. Don't think I am joking because with that bust in your hand I have justifiability to kill you. And who is that a bust of?" asked the officer.

She turned the bust around.

"It looks like Will", the alien leader's wife answered.

"You're actually going to destroy a valuable bust of your husband. How can you do such a thing? You are not a lady. You are an inhuman beast. I am going to kill you right now", said Officer Kerilic.

"Can I put the bust on the floor?" asked the alien leader's wife.

"Yes, you can. That doesn't mean I am not going to kill you. I am still going to kill you for using your husband's head to do something that I would fear you would do it for", answered Officer Kerilic.

"And how would you know what I am using my husband's head for?" asked Rubi.

"I wouldn't know but, I am assuming that you would either use him to smash the screen so that way I would lose the ability to kill you or denying you from entering the Secret Lair or that you would smash the light. Not only those two things but also, I'd feel you'd kill him because you don't like your husband at heart. So, that's the best thing you can to do to eradicate your husband to not get in any trouble with the law", answered the officer.

"You are absolutely wrong! In my defense and in truth, I am telling you that I would not want to eradicate my husband. You are the type to plant lies in me and you are good at twisting the facts. If you want to know the truth, I was going to use this to smash the screen so that way you wouldn't have the ability to kill me. I am doing this to save my own life because in this room I am defenseless. This is my only defense against a beast like you", replied the alien leader's wife.

"So, do I stand correct that you use your husband as a shield? As a human shield? So, if you were to go in combat during a war in Starmos City, you would hide behind your husband?" asked Officer Kerilic.

"No, I would be the one who would take the bullet if there was a war. I would rather die than my husband because he's actually worth more while than I am. He was the one who led the fight for justice against Cornelius. I wasn't. If my husband never existed, Starmos would remain under the socialist tyranny of Cornelius. My husband was the one who turned Starmos City into a complete 180 from a tyrannical, arbitrary, and unjust government to a fair, kind, honorable, chivalrous, respectable, and just government. He was the one who removed a one man leadership and made the leadership comprise of the parliamentary members and the senators. He was the one who taught the government to work in a bipartisan fashion. Cornelius didn't want any governing parties. Instead, he wanted the city to be under a one man rule, which was unfair and it did not progress the city in any way, shape, or form. He wasn't the one who fought for the citizens. He was the one who killed his dissidents. Will respects his dissidents. He only kills the ones who are trying to violate the rights of the citizens. Will puts the governed first before himself. He honors the governed. Unlike most democratic lands, he wants to ensure that he does not focus too much on the elections. Rather, he focuses on getting things done for his constituents. A lot of leaders of democratic lands probably invest more time in votes than leadership and fighting for the rights of the citizens. So, let me be clear to you. You have no rights to judge me based on my husband because I greatly admire my husband and he's one of the most inspirational folks that I look up to. My husband is an honorable and respectable individual. You are not", answered Rubi.

"Yeah, if you were trying to plea for mercy, you need to do a better job. I am extremely angry at you. You know why? You are being a phony. That's just typical of Rubi Von Alien", replied the officer.

He hit the laser button and shot the first bullet. The laser made a loud thud in the room. It is bouncing off the walls.

"What are you doing? Are you out of your damn mind?" asked Wilheim.

The laser is continuing to bounce off the walls. The laser disintegrated after thirty seconds of bouncing. Rubi and Wilheim jumped and tried to dodge the laser as much as possible.

"Are you crazy? Are you sick? Why are you doing such a thing?" the alien leader's wife asked.

"Because I can and I will fire another laser. So, you better watch out and you better be more agile because this laser is much bigger than the last one. It is going to take up practically this whole room", answered the officer.

The massive ray gun is five feet in diameter. The laser is four feet in diameter. The ray gun has three gold fins running across the top and four silver fins running across the sides. The fins are lighting up. The first two fins on the sides are lighting to show that the gun is working. The second two fins on the sides are showing the gun is turned on. The third side fins are showing the gun can be fired. The fourth fins show the gun is ready to launch the process. This is a very tense moment for both Rubi and Wilheim.

They are hiding underneath the screen. The first gold fin is lighting up. This gives the signal to show that the weapon is fully charged. The second one shows the ray is being created. The third one is showing the gun is about to be fired. The gun is speaking.

"T-10,-9,-8,-7,-6,-5,-4,-3,-2,-1. You are

dead."

Hearts are racing in the room. Although Rubi and Wilheim are hiding, it is extremely hard for them to avoid the bullet. The laser fired. It is bouncing off the walls. The moments are very tense. Both the alien leader's wife and cousin-in- law are tense in a deep corner. They are embracing each other, holding on for life. They are afraid the laser is about to hit them. The laser bounced to their corner and missed Wilheim by the skin of the teeth. The laser is bouncing back and forth. After thirty seconds of the laser traveling around the room, bouncing off the walls, the computer screen was hit. All of a sudden, a bright explosion took place. Officer Kerilic's evilness has been disabled so far. The alien leader's cousin fainted.

"What happened?" asked Rubi. The alien leader's cousin could not answer. "Wilheim. Wilheim! What happened to you?" she asked. Still, not any answer.

"Wilheim, wake up. I took you into this secret chamber because you need to come over here. It is scary what has been going on. I just saw a giant light explode in the room. I don't know what happened to you. Are you alive?" the alien leader's wife asked. A gasp of air left his body. His heart stopped.

"What was that?" asked Rubi.

He gasped again, except the gasp sounded more like a struggle for a breath of air.

"Are you okay? Will you come back? Can you breathe?" she asked. Still, not any answer. Another gasp of air was heard.

"Can you do me a favor and come back from the dead?" asked the alien leader's wife. "Yes", he answered with a struggle.

"What was that? Are you alive? Can you hear me? Do you know what I am asking you?" asked Rubi.

"Yes", Wilheim answered with another struggle.

"What was that?" the alien leader's wife asked.

"Yes", the alien leader's cousin answered.

He murmured, "for the third time", after answering, "yes."

"What was that?" asked Rubi.

The alien leader's cousin is becoming more audible.

"Yes, I am alive. I can hear you loud and clear. I just blanked out for a second."

"What?" the alien leader's wife asked.

"Are you stupid? Can you not understand what I am saying? It's not like I am speaking gibberish. I am speaking concisely in an audible manner. I am not speaking like an imbecile", answered Wilheim.

"Sorry, apparently, I am not able to understand gibberish. Thank God, you're alive", the alien leader's wife answered. "I am alive?" asked the alien leader's cousin.

"Of course, you're alive. If you weren't alive, you wouldn't be able to be speaking the way you're speaking. I know I am alive. I know I am not delusional either. Maybe that light made us go crazy. What do you think?" asked Rubi.

"Did you not realize you did all that talking to waste time? I simply said, 'I am alive?' Of course, I am alive. If I wasn't alive, I wouldn't be able to be speaking the way I did. I just wanted to get some stupid reaction out of you because I'd knew you react in an absurd manner when it came to a situation like this. Rubi, I know you're not intelligent. Don't even bother trying to make an argument with me. I was just trying to simply trick you. Wait! I wasn't even trying. It was quite easy for me to make a fool of you and guess what you did? You fell for it. Rubi, Rubi, Rubi", answered Wilheim.

He nodded his head after he answered

the question and crossed his two first index fingers.

"Hey, that's not nice. You're supposed to be respecting me. I was the one that brought you over to this Secret Lair. I can take you out of here. I was the one who was trying to help you in the situation you were in and you acted so disrespectful. How in all of the dimensions can you trick me like this? I am not supposed to be deceived. I am a Von Alien. Von Aliens are supposed to be intelligent and smart. Is that correct, Mr. Von Alien?" the alien leader's wife asked.

"Yes, that's correct. I am sorry for being such a smart ass. I didn't mean to be one. How about we handle things the mature way and not have such a quarrel over a ridiculous issue about who tricked who? How about you give me the chance to tell you about the secret that's going on in the Secret Lair", answered the alien leader's cousin.

"Why can't you tell me right here?" asked Rubi.

"Are these walls soundproof so that way the Parliamentary Hall cannot hear me?" asked Wilheim.

"No, I don't think so. How come the walls have to be soundproof in order for you to tell me what you must tell me?" asked the alien leader's wife.

"I am going to tell you later. For now, let's focus on getting out of here. I think it'd be important that we find another room before Kerilic fires a massive laser, where we and the entire room are destroyed", answered Wilheim.

"And how do you expect us to get out of here when those double doors are sealed shut?" asked Rubi.

"Simple. Do you have that bust with you?" the alien leader's cousin asked.

"What bust are you talking about?" the alien leader's wife asked.

"How can you not remember? The bust that you were carrying. The bust of your husband Will. You were going to use that bust to smash the countdown clock on the double doors. I need you to open those doors now", answered Wilheim.

"In the light explosion, I think I acquired some form of amnesia where I kind of lost my mind. So, you need to give me some info to let me have some recollection of what went on", replied the alien leader's wife.

"I understand that, but do you not realize that none of us can have a form of amnesia, even when an issue like this takes place. We need to have some form of psychological remembrance. Our recollection abilities must be put to use. Therefore, we must be able to remember past events because our past affects our future. They say, '*everyday you make your history*.' That stands to be the absolute truth. And over the course of the past six months, we have made tremendous history and we still have a way to go", answered Wilheim.

"Good, I get your point. I need to be able to recall more information. I will try and think more. Yeah, I believe it's more important to think than to act in a quixotic and impetuous fashion. We will learn to get things done the way they should get done. And that's through thinking and rationale", replied Rubi.

"Great, now you get the hang of it. So, where's the bust?" the alien leader's wife asked.

She walked from the corner to the center of the room, where the bust was located. She is looking on the floor panicking. She's checking her pockets. The bust is not in her pockets. She's looking frantically all across the room from corner to corner, wall to wall, and across the screen.

"The Bust! Where is it? It must've disintegrated", she said nervously.

She is still looking in the room. "Perhaps, I should check my pockets", Wilheim nonchalantly replied.

He searched his pockets.

"It's not here. What should we do? How are we going to get out of here?" the alien leader's wife asked nervously. "We will get out of here in a calm fashion", answered the alien leader's cousin.

"Calm? Calm? Calm? Are you serious? Are you stupid? Are you absurd? This is not a calm situation. We might be stuck here and if Officer Kerilic manages to fix the computer system, he might consider firing another laser. We might not make it through this one. Then, this won't be good. We will be dead, dead, dead! Do you want that to happen? Are you out of your mind? Are you sick just like he is?" asked Rubi.

"I am not sick at all. I think you're the one who's sick right now. Why are you acting so fearful. Maybe, you should learn to listen and if you listen, you'll learn", answered Wilheim.

"Are you saying 'I am stupid?' Do you think I am unintelligent? Do you not think I can handle this situation on my own?" the alien leader's wife answered.

"Absolutely not. You are not able to handle this situation for you are freaking out and acting irrationally. I was taught if you are in such a harsh situation, you do something what is called 'problem solving' and thinking with intellect, which you clearly do not possess. You might possess intellect but, you don't possess problem solving. If you want to problem solve, you'll just do what I'll do. You'll let me slam my fist against the countdown clock", replied Wilheim.

"What's the sense in doing that?" asked Rubi.

"Well, do you happen to see the countdown clock working?" asked the alien leader's cousin.

"I don't see it working right now. Do you think slamming your fist against something not working will make it work. Do you think you'll be able to let us out of this uncomfortable space by simply hitting this clock. I can do it. Do you want to see me do it?" the alien leader's wife asked.

"Yes, I do. If you think you're super strong, then prove it to me. This clock is meant to be struck by a man's hand. So, I think you should keep your lady like hands off the clock", answered Wilheim.

"Who are you calling a lady?" asked Rubi.

"I am calling you a lady because you're

elegant and gentle hands like yours are not supposed to hit such massive objects", answered the alien leader's cousin.

"Come here", said the alien leader's wife.

Wilheim walked up to her. She slapped him on the right cheek and he fell to the floor. THUD. "That's what happens when you underestimate the strength of a woman. Don't ever mess with a woman. Don't underestimate the strength of Rubi", replied Rubi. She walked up to the countdown clock and jumped up. She slapped the clock.

She screamed. A light BANG was heard on the floor. BANG. BANG. BANG. Her teeth are clenched.

"OMG, I can't stand the pain I'm in. It's just extremely uncomfortable. I'm sorry, Wilheim. I didn't mean to slap you like that. You didn't deserve it. I am sorry that I thought I knew everything. I don't know everything. I may have intellect but, I don't have any common sense. I'll listen to you when it comes to opening up passage ways for us to have access to. I am just sorry. I don't know how to put this in any other words. I am just here to simply say, 'I am sorry'.", she said.

"Very Good. It's fine. You don't have to be so melodramatic. You just have to be less myopic and more aware. Let me be very clear though. I want to tell you that this is what you have to do. I will clench my hand into a fist and slam the marquis. This will cause the door to open and then we will be safe. We will be able to move on with our journey and I will be able to tell you the secret that is necessary to be told", replied the alien leader's cousin.

He walked to the back of the room, ran, and jump about five feet in the air. As he was jumping, he slammed his fists against the countdown clock.

"Who is to damage me?" asked the clock.

The clock's voice is that of Officer Kerilic's.

"Open the door, now! I mean it! I will kill you if you don't open the door. I know exactly who you are! I hereby demand you open the door", declared Wilheim.

"Who do you think you are?"

"I am Miles Blanco", answered the alien leader's cousin.

He is lying through his teeth. Officer Kerilic managed to open the double doors. The alien leader's wife and her cousin-in-law entered the metallic paneled room. This room is made of aluminum panels. There are 7 uneven panels on all four walls, the ceiling, and the floor. There's a light imbedded in the ceiling. The alien leader's cousin and Rubi slowly entered the room.

The double doors behind them closed.

"What's in this room?" asked Rubi.

"You should know. Have you not been in this room before?" asked Wilheim.

"Yes, like I said, I had amnesia earlier", answered the alien leader's wife.

"Didn't I say earlier that neither one of us can afford to have amnesia nor can we not be able to have any form of intellect? We must have both recollection and intellect. We must be in touch with reality", replied the alien leader's cousin.

"True that", said Rubi.

"You're right. That is totally true. Now, I need to deal with this", replied the alien leader's cousin.

"You're one hundred percent right", the alien leader's wife said.

"Good, I believe we just said that earlier", replied Wilheim.

"Yes", said Rubi.

Wilheim is staring at the walls and he's walking in a trance, where he appears to be unconsciously thinking. He is pacing around the room, being oblivious to the corners. He keeps slamming himself into corners after two paces around the room. He stopped slamming into corners after thirty seconds of pacing. After, one minute, he is feeling the walls for some bizarre reason. Rubi is looking at him in a skeptical manner.

She is just staring at him pacing around the room in shock. At the same time, she is also questioning psychologically why he is doing such a thing. The alien leader's cousin is still feeling the walls. Rubi, is still standing in the middle of the room. After twenty paces and touches around the walls, Wilheim is still feeling the walls and pacing. Rubi is spinning trying to follow the direction he is moving. She spun all the way to the dead center of the room. She is still spinning.

Her head is losing it. She fell to the floor and vomited after spinning for a while. Wilheim is still walking around the room. He is evaluating the walls. From feeling the walls, he is now banging them. Rubi awakened from her amnesia.

"What's going on? Are you out of your mind?" she asked.

Wilheim is still walking around the room nonchalantly banging on the walls.

"Why are you banging on the walls?" she asked.

The alien leader's cousin is ignoring Rubi. She reiterated the question verbatim. After thirty seconds of refusal to answer the question, she walked in front of Wilheim.

"What are you doing? Why are you pacing like crazy? Why are you banging on the walls? Is there something wrong with you, perhaps?" the alien leader's wife asked.

He did not answer that question. Anger is starting to show in Rubi's face. Her blue skin is turning red, although it looks purple. Her eyes are squinted and her lips are tight. Some parts of her light lipstick fell off her mouth. Her hair is becoming frizzy. She bluntly stood in the way of Wilheim. He walked around her.

"Why are you pacing and making this annoying racket of noise? Do you realize that your banging on the walls is an absurdity and a disgrace? Don't make such stupid noises.. One should not make ridiculous noise like this. It is an absurdity. You are not acting intelligent like you tout yourself to be. You are acting like a looney tune. Would you please stop?" the alien leader's wife asked nicely.

He is still doing the absurd action that he has been doing for the past five minutes. She returned back to the middle of the room. She is studying his action and analyzing it. She is speaking to herself in an aside.

"I wonder why he is doing this. Is he doing this to be immature? Or act absurd? Is he doing this to annoy me or to aggravate me? Is he doing this because he wants to know something? I don't think there's anything for him to know. I hope he doesn't think I am crazy because I'm talking to myself. Some folks may think I am just plain crazy because of this. I bet you think I am plain crazy", she said in an aside.

She is acting in an odd manner. Once again, she walked in front; of him. He is still pacing. After ten minutes of pacing, he's starting to become dizzy. In his viewpoint, the room looks like it is rotating. He started walking in a wobbly manner. He is walking on the side of his right leg in a limp.

Rubi kicked him. "Stop it! I am telling you to cut the shenanigans out! I don't know why you are acting the way you're acting but, whatever you're doing, you better stop. And I mean it. This is an absurdity. You shouldn't be pacing around the room unnecessarily. I have been asking you the same question, not once, not twice, not three times, not four times, but five times. I have been simply asking you, 'What are you doing?' Pacing around a room is not typical unless you are going through a cathartic venting of pent up emotional energy, if you are physically energetic, if you're on the phone, if you're angry, or if you are trying to figure out something. Those should be the only reasons why you're pacing around the room. Wilheim, I don't think your cousin, Will, would want you to act like that. I don't think your parents would want you to act like that. And I certainly don't want you to act like that. Wilheim, you are better than that. You are a great man. Although, I won't love you as much as I love my husband you are one of the folks that I like to be with. I just want to know why you are acting the way you have been acting. Can you please tell me?" asked the alien leader's wife.

She is pleading for him to give her an answer. He is trying to blink his eyes. Wilheim has been unconscious while Rubi was speaking to him regarding his past action. The slow blinking of his eyes increased within a matter of ten seconds. His eye blinking is now increasing. He is blinking at one thousand blinks per millisecond. He is blinking at an extremely fast speed. His eyes became very weak.

"My Eyes! My Eyes! What;s going on with my eyes?" he asked.

"It looks like your eyes are having some sort of involuntary movement. Maybe you should relax and calm down. You were in a ten minute trance of pacing around the room, tapping on the walls, and then banging on the walls. You were acting crazy. What was that about?" the alien leader's wife asked.

"Why are you asking me this particular question? I was pacing around the room for a couple of reasons. Somehow, it ended up in some sort of a crazy trance", the alien leader's cousin answered.

"Well, I want to know the two reasons. Can you please just give me the two reasons why you were pacing around the room acting in an absurd manner?" asked Rubi.

"Okay, I will give you the two reasons. I don't think this is the Secret Lair. I think there's more to this lair than meets the eye. This lair should have way more than this small room. There should be more to this lair. So, I was trying to figure out the way to get to the rest of this lair. Second of all, I was pacing around the room to burn off some calories. I am pretty overweight, although I don't look it, I think I would burn a few calories through doing what I did. Somehow, when one is doing the same activity over, over, and over again, that causes somebody to end up in a trance or it causes a habit. For me, I ended up in a trance, involuntarily got dizzy, and fainted. Don't worry something like this will never happen again. To prevent a fight between you and I, we will just drop the fact that I ended up in a trance doing the crazy thing of pacing around the room and I will never be able to do such a thing again if I am more aware. I was self-critical and I took accountability for my actions. I won't act like a clown again. I won't do anything to the point where I'll have to have the attention smacked or kicked into me. Rubi, please forgive me for I have wronged you. I want to be respectful and I should be ashamed of myself", answered Wilheim.

"Why are you getting so melodramatic? What got me angry was that you were pacing and ignoring me. I was trying to ask you a couple of simple questions regarding your actions and I felt you were refusing to answer me because you kept moving along in your trance. I didn't realize you were in a trance. I should've prevented you from ending up in such a trance and unconscious action by hitting the button a long time ago. I was just trying to see if you would be able to figure out where the button is located. I wanted to see if you had the intellect that you claim you had. As a result, you don't. Do you realize that you made yourself look absurd by pacing around the room and slamming the walls? I think you were acting absurd and I deliberately made you act like that because you were condescending to me earlier when I felt my amnesia. Don't worry. I won't be having an amnesia issue only if you do me one big favor. Don't end up in a crazy trance. Stop pacing. Don't do that ever again. You will behave well. Wilheim, in spite of this, you are a great man. Although, I don't see we're in a fight. I can see where you're going with the secret you have to tell me. I don't want to know the secret until I tell you. First thing's first, we will be going on a tour of the Secret Lair. Then, you will tell me what the issue is or what you like to call your secret. Then, we will take care of the issue like we should. I want to ensure this process is quick. We will ensure that this process is done in a just fashion", said Rubi. "You are absolutely right. You've brought up some very good and quite important points", replied the alien leader's cousin.

Chapter IV: The First Ordeal: The Beginning Of The Secret Lair

It is now about half past six in the evening. The alien leader's cousin and Rubi are in the possible gateway to the entrance of the way to the Secret Lair. The alien leader's wife retrieved one of the metallic panels. Underneath the massive four by four panel, is a complex control box. On the Upper left corner is the power button for the Alien Estate.

The power button is a one foot lever. Adjacent to the lever, is a large amount of lights. These lights are incessantly flickering. The orange lights come in the form of two inches in diameter. They look like orange buttons except they are unpushable. There are twelve rows of six power buttons on each row. All of the buttons are labeled.

The first row shows that the outlets are working. The first outlet shows the label microwave oven outlet. The second one shows the fridge outlet. The third shows the kitchen stove one. The fourth shows the blender/ juicer source. The fifth shows the night light power source. The sixth one shows the phone charger outlet. Then, the second row shows all the outlets for the parlor room and the dinette. The first three outlets are for the dinette.

Floor one and floor two outlets are imbedded in the floor. These outlets are there in case there's an event that requires using the floor's electricity. There's the back light outlet. In the parlor room, there are a few outlets. The first outlet shows shelf lights. The second one shows window lights. The third one shows Spotlights. The fourth one shows couch lights.

Then, there are Will's bedroom's outlets. The first two show those that are in the powder. The first one shows the soda machine. The second one shows the hairdryer plug. Then, the rest of the outlets are in the bedroom, itself. There's the television outlet, the closet, the lampstand and the Dresser Outlet. The next row shows the alien leader's wife and Light's bedroom. In Rubi's Bedroom, there are three outlets. There's the dresser outlet and two lamp outlets. Lights Bedroom shows the presence of three outlets. There's the charger outlet. Adjacent to the label, charger outlet, one hundred gigawatts to be used on a nightly basis. There's the lamp outlets and dresser outlets.

Adjacent to Light's and Rubi's row of outlets, there's the guest bedroom outlets. There are six outlets dominating the guest bedroom.

The north and south outlets, the night light, the television, the bed outlet, and the leisure outlet. The next row shows the label of hallway outlets. There are the north right, north left, and north center outlets, which dominate the first three lights in this row.

Below those lights, are the second three lights. There are the south right, south left, and south center outlets. Both the south and north center outlets are located underneath two tables. These tables are used to hold plants. Then, there's the row for the outdoor outlets.

The outlets in this particular row show the fountain outlet, two of the outlets in this row belong to the planter lights, then there are three driveway outlets for charging LSCs that are not Light. The next six outlets show the backyard outlets. The first two lights on this side of the panel belong to the grill and the pool. There's the fan outlet let for the patio.

There's the heater outlet and the pool vacuum outlet. Furthermore, there's the outlet for the Luna Wicker Daybed. The next row of lights belong to the outlets on the grass in front of the Alien Estate. This group of lights are labeled G.O. and in numerical order from one to six. The next group of lights are labeled the air outlets.

When the airshow of Starmos City takes place for the model planes, the outlets are used to charge the planes the day before the event takes place. These outlets are also listed in numerical order from one to six. The tenth and eleventh rows are used for the grass has outlets to host the band concerts. The final group of outlets are labeled dining room lights. The top two lights are labeled for the outlets for the china closets, that being their lights. The middle two lights are used for the back outlets, which are predominantly used to warming the trays for the Hors D'Oueveres.

Then, the last two lights are used for the outlets that are featured in front of the window. These outlets are rarely used unless there's a special concert taking place. Adjacent to the outlets, on the circuit board, is the switchboard. There are approximately nineteen switches, one for each room of the estate. There are three rows of switches, two hold seven and one holds five.

All the labels on the switchboard are mentioned with labels. The first row of switches show the power sources for the first level of the Alien Estate. The following switches on the first row show: Will's bedroom, Light's bedroom, Rubi's bedroom, The guest room, dining room, kitchen, and dining/ parlor room. The second row shows the switches and their labels of the following: The right parliamentary tables, the center parliamentary tables, left parliamentary tables, the throne, the Secret Lair, the library door, and Parliament Hall's lights. The third row shows the switches for the exterior of the estate of the following: the driveway lights, the lawn lights, the fountain, The backlights of the estate, and the patio electricity.

Below the switchboard is the water meter. There are red and green lights for the water meter. All the lights on the water meter are green. There are six pumps. There's the sewage pump on the top, the kitchen pump on the bottom, laundry pump in the middle; above the laundry pump, is the bathroom water pump; and below the bathroom water pump, is the kitchen water pump.

The warmth and coolness are determined by the one, who is turning the valves. When a light is red, that means the pump is not functioning or there must be a water main break. The water main break took place when Starmos City was first established. If one wonders why there are mountains around the city, it's because they were man made because this city is located below sea level.

One would have the illusion that he or she is in the middle of a desert in the orange mountains of Starmos City. However, that individual is wrong. Adjacent to the pump lights are the transportation tracks and lights. This is the first part of the board that is not used for the estate. These lights are used for the Starmos Train Station. There are blue, white, and yellow lights used for this system. The blue lights are used to determine where the train is departing.

The white lights mean the train is currently located at the train station.

The yellow lights mean that a train is cancelled. There are labels to identify the numbers of the trains. #1 means the train is heading either East Bound or North Bound. #2 means the train is heading either West Bound or South Bound. #3 means the train is either heading Northwest or Southwest. #4 means the train is heading Northeast. #5 means the train is heading Southeast. #6 is a special number determined for the form of transportation within Starmos City. Below these boards are the street boards. The street boards are colored the universal colors of a street light. All the roads are traffic free.

There are thirty three lights. There are three lights for each of the eleven streets in the city. Fortunately, all the lights are green. This means the roads are perfect. The yellow means your ride might be hindered slightly. Generally, the lights for the roads are either green or yellow. It is rare to see a red light. This is the only item that is dependent on a mixture between computerized technology and satellites. Adjacent to this is the Emergency Intercom System.

This only takes place in case of an invasion of the city where there's an evacuation of all the citizens if such an event ever has to take place. All of the systems are dependent on a computer system, which is one of the key components, which keeps this city functioning comfortably and safely. Although there were plenty of invasions of this city, there were never any incidences where one would have to use this area. There's only one way the power can be turned off legitimately. The only way the power can be turned off is in the hands of the alien leader. He has to be approved by the Senate and Parliament.

From there, the citizens have to make an approval, and then, the alien leader can decide after receiving the approval from the Parliamentary Hall and referendum from the citizens. He has never done this, and he would have to tap is eyes against a screen, which can determine if he will be able to make the move. He will have to place his hands on a fingerprint scanner. Wilheim is staring at this device in awe.

"It's amazing how complex this area is especially with this circuit board being here. You live in a marvelous estate. You live in such a technologically innovative place. Do you realize what you have here?" he asked.

"Oh, yes. This circuit board determines all the mundane and prose activities that take place in Starmos City. This is not something marvelous. Any home can have such a device if a home is this complex. Although half of this device is used for this house, for which we are gathered in, the other half is used to manage the flow of the city. If you want to turn off the electricity, then you can do it right here by turning this lever. Come on, do it", Rubi answered with a smile.

"Are you sure about this?" the alien leader's cousin asked.

"Yes, sure. Why not? It's not like you'll be shocked", answered the alien leader's wife.

She put her hand above the *Not* in the warning sign. The warning sign states. *Warning! Do not touch. You will be shocked.* Wilheim is reading the red lettered white background sign.

"But, Rubi, it says, 'Warning. Do not touch.' I'll get shocked if I touch it. Do you think I want to be eletrocuted? I can assure you that I can't afford to get shocked. It's not going to be good. Do you realize I can be paralyzed if such a thing happens to me? I can't afford to go through such an issue. Just please don't make me feel compelled to pull the lever", he said. "No, buddy, I don't think you know how to read. What it really says is, you can touch it. It's just that you'll be shocked in great amazement. It looks phenomenal. Imagine, you have control over this city with this lever. Do you want to be able to control the city with this? Wilheim, the power rests in your hands. Will is not down here. He won't know it's you who's doing it", the alien leader's wife said.

In an aside, she told herself, "I don't care if Will finds out. I know it's not going to be me. He'll know I am trying to stop him. If he knows this, I will be able to cause trouble and he won't know about it. Wilheim is so stupid and gullible. He can't even read the sign clearly. His decision to fail to read the sign the right way is going to cause him his fate. I mean his fate of joy."

He is reaching the lever slowly. His hands are shaking. He is sweating making a large project out of pulling a simple lever. His body is trembling as he is holding onto the lever. He feels excited to retrieve control over Starmos City. At the same time, his innate conscious is telling him not to touch the lever.

In spite of his conscious trying to kick in, he took twenty seconds to pull the lever down. The power of the city turned off. All of a sudden, a pen started submerging down from the ceiling. This pen is blue and there are lightning rods beaming back and forth. The laser point is hitting Wilheim. Completely unaware of what's about to take place against him, he is looking at Rubi. He is staring at her in skepticism.

"Neither am I shocked literally nor am I surprised. I don't think I'm going to get electrocuted So, you were wrong this whole time", he said.

"Are you stupid enough that you wouldn't be able to see what I was doing? When

I was telling you to read that sign. I covered my hand on the word *not*. You should've realized that. I was deceiving you the whole time. I think you should not look above you right now because something really good is going to happen", she replied. He didn't look up at the Electrocution Pen. The shock noise in the pen is being made. "What's that?" he asked.

"It's your ultimate death", answered the alien leader's wife. He looked up.

"Oh shit! I am dead", he screamed.

The pen released the electricity. He is being electrocuted. Smoke is emerging from his ears. His head is turning red. His hair is on fire. The blue shirt is burning. He is wide-eyed, unaware of what's happening against him. He is basically destroyed.

His body started moving from a straight manner into an undulating manner. He is levitating from the ground and turning green. Rubi is laughing in a ridiculous and absurd manner. Her behavior is extremely draconian because she is a supposed supporter of Wilheim and her husband.

If she believes in protecting some folks, she should believe in protecting Wilheim. His electrocution was finished. The top of the ceiling is moving upward. A red siren started to emerge from the ceiling and an alarm noise is being made. This alarm noise sounds like an out of tune sounding gong. BONG, BONG, BONG, BONG!

The alarm is making extremely loud noises. This noise is continuing to take place until the Alien Estate security is entering. The alien leader's cousin is struggling to stand. He is speechless because his larynx was negatively affected by the horrible and sudden shock.

The alien leader's wife, Rubi, is looking at Wilheim with disregard. For thirty seconds, she looked at the wall disregarding the electrocuted cousin. She turned around.

"Oh, do you need help?" she asked in a soft voice.

"Yes, get me a stretcher and a hair dryer. Keep me dry. Being wet is going to keep me more in shock. I am going to be unfortunately stuck in this state for a few minutes. Don't touch me", the alien leader's cousin answered.

"How come? Don't you want me to rescue you?" Rubi asked.

Her demeanor is very condescending, dishonest, and not genuine.

"Yes, I do; but touching me is not going to rescue me. I need you to send some medical professionals to come down here so I can not die. I already feel like I am dying. Do you want me to die?" asked Wilheim.

"Oh, no. I don't want you to die. In fact, I'd rather be the one electrocuted than you being the one. Why should you be the one who's electrocuted? You didn't live your life. I did. I had a better life than you did because I've been living with my husband for many years. You must be the one that lives. I'd rather be shocked than you. I think you should not survive", the alien leader's wife answered in a sarcastic and snide manner.

A smirk is shown on her face and she clearly showed that facial expression to Wilheim. He thinks she is trying to help him. He is losing shock.

"I think you are being way too nice to me. What have I done for you that made you think I was this nice person.? All I've done for you was be a hindrance. You were the one who did things for me. So, you have a right to live. I don't deserve to live. All I have done was fight against Cornelius unsuccessfully. I need to be the one who's improved. Maybe that shock did me some good. You don't need to sacrifice yourself, for you are a great woman. Rubi, you have a husband. I don't have a wife. You have a city to run. I have a house to run. You have to help manage a government. I have to help manage my job and my house. You have to travel different places. I don't have to travel different places. You are directly affected by foreign invaders along with your husband. I am affected by my own actions and those of the government. I am not as meaningful as you are. I am just the common-folk. I am just somebody who is an average citizen trying to make something of himself in a newly formed democracy. I wasn't as relentless in the fight for democracy as your husband was. You were working along with your husband who fought for justice, who fought for democracy, who fought against tyranny. Neither, do I deserve to die nor should I be the first one to run from death", replied Wilheim.

The alien leader's wife scoffed and laughed. "You know something? Let me tell you that this is the first time, you actually made sense. My life does deserve to be spared. I shouldn't be the one in shock. I shouldn't be the fallen sow. Rather, I should be the strong Lion. And I am the strong Lion. I was the one who fought for justice against the tyranny of Cornelius. Not only did I do that, but I also fought for strengthening our borders against foreign invaders. What did you do? Nothing. You didn't do anything for the good of the citizens of this city. You only did things for the good of yourself. That's just typical of you. You are an individual who does not care about anybody else but yourself. You should be ashamed", the alien leader's wife said.

Wilheim is regaining clear

consciousness.

"I told you those nice comments not to butter you up, but to be very honest with you. I didn't want to say I did anything meaningless because those who work hard do meaningful things and may those who work hard go far. Those folks shall prosper. Now, I have not said, 'you should live longer than I have simply because I am not as productive as you are. I didn't say I deserve to die.' Yet, you believe that. I praised you on why you should live. You shouldn't tell me that I am this meaningless individual. I am somebody who's trying to make something of himself in this city. Now, because you were acting arrogant to me, I will now act bold to you and challenge your beliefs. First of all, what gives you the right to ridicule me? No, I am not a politician. No, I am not in the same political level as you are. And no, I am not somebody who is trying to seek political. office as of yet. Secondly, I am not condescending like you are. You like to ridicule one based on his or her financial or career status. I have respect for you. I never scoffed at you like you've scoffed at me. I never insulted you based on your job description, which is to be nothing but a figurehead. If you want to criticize me based on my job, I will criticize you based on your job. You tout yourself that because you are Will's wife, you think you have the prerogative to do whatever you want. Tax does not come out of your salary. And gold-digging mooches like you are the causes of all the trouble in this city. Rubi, maybe you need to start being nicer. That reminds me. Thirdly, you need to learn to stop scoffing and ridiculing me. I am somebody who's trying to become successful in this city. I am trying to improve the quality of life in this city. Instead of calling me a self-centered, self-aggrandizing, self- righteous individual, maybe you should call me an individual, who is not a mooch like you are, somebody who is not a bullshit artist like you are claiming that you live in a boxcar, and somebody who is a kiss-up to your husband. Let me tell you something, I am very honest with you. Rubi, I have respect and honor for you. You are a kind woman. I do not have any idea for what has taken place today. You are a lovable individual. Maybe, this being the First Lady Of Starmos City is not working out for you. Rubi, I love you for who you are as a woman. However, your attitude must stop. Being that I am Will's cousin, being that you helped me when I was down, alerted me when I was not awake, and you were there for me in this long, but yet, short ordeal. Rubi, you are a perfect woman. Neither am I a terribly flawed man nor am I, a perfectionist. I am somebody who is the average Starmos City citizen, who is just trying to get by in life. Now, my cousin, Will, lived in the estate half of his entire lifespan. He moved in due to an unfortunate situation. Cornelius killed his parents simply because the parents were dissidents. That was wrong. Rubi, he thought who he was and you saw what happened to him. Do you want the same thing to happen to you where you'll get shot?" the alien leader's cousin asked.

"Absolutely, not. I thought the kiss-up game was over. I think kissing up to some folks is wrong. Quite frankly, let me retract that comment. I think to most folks it is wrong. Of course, you should act like a kiss-up to your boss, but I think that's pretty much the only man who you'd kiss up to. You kissed up to me, which I didn't like. Wilheim you are the one who needs to be kinder especially right now that you're in a glass house and somebody's about to throw a rock at that house. Now, I want to discuss the secret with you. It's quite important that you tell me your secret", the alien leader's wife answered.

"I don't want to sound like I have had audacious behavior. However, we were both kissing up to each other. That's not right. And when I said earlier my life is not important as your life, I meant it. However, I did not believe I should die. I am too good to die", answered Wilheim.

The alarms are still wailing. The alarms are still making boisterous noise. The alien leader's cousin is covering his ears.

"Why are you covering your ears?" asked Rubi.

Wilheim's face of anger is showing. He would never typically be angry with her.

However, he is starting to understand her true side. He is staring at her wide-eyed. About thirty seconds later, he squinted his eyes. His hands are clenched in fists.

"What's wrong with you?" the alien leader's cousin asked hoarsely and brusquely.

"Who do you think you are to get angry with me? I was the one who put you on the list to come into this lair. You have no right to speak to me like that. You are lucky to be with me in this lair. You are lucky to be with me in the Alien Estate. You are lucky to be in this dimension. You are lucky to be alive. This is audacious behavior on your part. Anybody who was just added on this list has not a single right to show any disrespect and from what I recalled, you were the one who was just added on the list not too long ago. Don't worry we can have a reversal of that. If you want that to take place, we can have such a thing arranged. Quite frankly, I wouldn't care if that took place. All I care about is myself and Will", the alien leader's wife answered.

"What kind of a woman are you? Rather, I meant, what kind of lady are you? How can you treat one your guests on the list with utter disrespect. Let me tell you something. You are not a supporter of Will. If you were a supporter of Will, you would not act the way you are acting. Your behavior is not acceptable. Secondly, you are not an individual who is kind.

You are somebody who is an evil individual. All you want to do is cause trouble. You have tried to electrocute me and that was deliberately. You weren't the one who pulled the lever. I was. That's a truth that we both cannot disagree with. Was it correct that you were the one who told me to do such a thing? Theretofore, I cannot stand up comfortably. I am struggling to stand. That is insensitive. It's one thing to joke around. It's another thing to say, 'you're joking around' and to be a volatile individual. Rubi, you are not the fellow that I thought you were. There's another side to you that I don't know. You are the devil in disguise. You shall be punished for being that way. You are calling me arrogant and self-centered when I am clearly not that. If I was arrogant and self-centered, I am somebody who would not care about your life or about the bust of your husband. Officer Kerilic was right earlier. You are self-centered, although, I shouldn't; say his actions are right", Wilheim replied with disgust.

"You do not have to tell me that I am insensitive. I will tell you why. I am not insensitive. I was somebody who fought for the folks of Starmos City. I fought for their independence from Cornelius. I just don't like you. I am not self- centered in the house because I am somebody that actually does give a crap about my husband. You don't have a wife because you are incompatible. You can't live with her because you will behave in a disrespectful manner. You have disrespected a wonderful woman who helped fight for the justice for the folks of Starmos City. Wilheim, who is to say you are not going to disrespect and be disdainful towards a woman in your own house? You are already showing disdain for somebody who has more authority than you do. Wait. I forgot. You have absolutely no authority whatsoever. You are somebody who is not a fighter. You are a quitter. Quite frankly, you do not deserve to be living. You are an alien who is not here to make something of himself. You are a nothing. You are a scrub. You have absolutely no significance in this city", said Rubi.

"What is a scrub?", the alien leader's cousin asked.

"It is an insignificant individual. It is a slang term. And that's what you are", the alien leader's wife answered.

"A slang term. Por Que?" asked Wilheim.

"Do you mistake me for a fool? I know what Por Que means.

It means 'Why?", answered Rubi.

"Rubi, you are an insignificant individual and a nothing. You are a nonproductive member of society. You tout yourself to be this wonderful woman who is here to benefit society. Meanwhile, you don't know how to benefit your own house, for you are volatile. I can tell by your demeanor that you are out to destroy your husband's career. If you are going to deny what I've just told you, you're absolutely wrong. I \am not somebody who is out to destroy my cousin's reputation. I am here to help him. Rubi, knowing you, you probably want your husband to die so you can run Starmos City. Although this is not a monarchy, I am sure if the citizens didn't know your evil side, you would be elected with probably 80% of the vote. I don't want you to be voted in because you'll be like Jacqueline. I bet you are making your husband write his will and have it arranged for you to inherit all the material. That kind of behavior is not acceptable", argued the alien leader's cousin.

She is walking to the back of the wall. She lunged at him. Her hands are pushed outward in cuffed position. She is ready to choke her cousin-in-law. Her adrenaline is high. She is sweating and grunting. She is choking him. He is turning purple. He can barely speak.

"You're an evil piece of garbage", the alien leader's cousin struggled to say.

His skin is turning an indigo color. All of a sudden noises are being heard from the stairs of Parliamentary Hall. The footsteps sound like those of large crowd. The library door opened. Screams in the background are being heard. An upper level man is saying, "Move it.

Move it. Brigade, enter. You must enter this room. There's trouble. Do not halt at any point. Remember, this is not reconnaissance. This is an attack on the estate! You can't afford to stop", said the military leader.

There are about fifty troops entering the room. All of the troops are running. All have the flat top haircuts. Their skins are blue like that majority of all the alien citizens. They have a navy colored uniform. The hats of different officers have sowings of flags based on their ranking. The top level ranking is represented by zig-zag lines. There are two lines with two zig-zags on each line.

The colors of these lines are dark red for the Bravery Title. The upper middle level ranking is represented by a white filled in circle with a gold star in the center. This upper middle level ranking means one is a Strong Enforcer. The center ranking has a green coat of arms. The green coat of arms means one is chivalrous during any military ventures.

The lower middle ranking means one is an Adroit Observer. This ranking is represented by a silhouette of a Hawk. The lowest ranking is a Private. This ranking has two swords intersecting each other at the center. These swords mean one is willing to jump on the front lines.

All the troops here belong to the Private

Ranking and one of the troops belongs to the ranking of a Hawk, that troop being the lesser general. All of the military men are wearing black boots with laces on the sides. The laces are tied in a surgical knot. Despite them being tied in a surgical knot, the troop can slip the shoe on and off comfortably.

The surgical knot is used to represent the unification of Starmos City especially the military within the city. All the military men carry shackles in case they come across a wanted felon. All of them carry guns, most of whom carry handguns. ten out of the fifty troops are carrying semiautomatic machine guns, ready to fire.

The troops are chanting, "We must fight! We must fight! We must fight for justice!"

They are chanting this as they are marching to where the lever was pulled. Wilheim is cowering in fear laying on the floor. Rubi, is on top of him choking him. The troops stopped. The general stopped.

"Why are you choking this man?" he asked.

"Because I can", the alien leader's wife answered.

"Well, do you realize I can arrest you for behaving in such a despicable and atrocious manner?" asked the general.

"You can't arrest me. I am the President's Wife", answered Rubi.

"So what? Does the President's Wife think she's above the law? Can she be above the law according to the Constitution?" asked the general.

She smirked. "Yes, they can. Of course, anybody in high political office is above the law and shall not therefore, be held responsible", she answered.

"You saw what happened to Cornelius and Jacqueline. What makes you think the same thing is not going to happen to you? Just because you think you're Rubi, who supposedly fought for democracy does not mean you are above the law. You are far from being above the law", replied the general.

"I guess you're right general. I am too far from being above the law. So, can you please tell me what's wrong?" the alien leader's wife asked.

A sinister smirk is seen on her face as Wilheim is gasping for air.

"Yes, I think the scene is quite obvious. You're trying to choke him. I don't know the exact reason why; but I'd think it be important if you told me. Wait a minute. Did I say I think? I meant, you better tell me or else I have every right to shoot you right now", said the general.

"What gives you the right to shoot the alien leader's wife? You know, I can have you charged for making a threat. You are accusing me of being above the law, but, yet you think you're above the law by claiming you have the carte blanche to shoot me. That's not the case, my friend. There's not any such thing as having carte blanche to kill somebody", argued Rubi.

"I think you're wrong. I have a right to shoot anybody who's violating the law and who can harm others. I have the right to shoot anybody who chooses to commit or attempt to commit a homicide on the spot. I have those rights because I'm a general. Now, this whole thing will be over if you can explain to me exactly why your choking him. Please, can you explain?" asked the general.

He has a foreign accent when he speaks. VALENCIA is written on the top of his badge. He is still bald and a little overweight. He still has the raspy voice.

"Who are you to tell me to explain myself for such an action? I can do whatever I want. I married Will. Neither your family nor your friends married my husband. I'll call him down here right now if I have to, and he'll take care of you. He will take you out. And not in the dinner sense. He will beat the living daylights out of you. So, let me be perfectly clear, you better watch yourself and what you are doing", said the alien leader's wife. "Listen, lady. I just want an answer from you. I want you to tell me why you're choking him. Can you please tell me?" asked General Valencia.

"Because I saw him pulling the lever. I'd figured he had malicious intent to shut down the electricity in Starmos City. I was afraid he was doing that for that reason. I was afraid he was going to gain control over this city. I know exactly his motive. He was trying to take control. And so in order to take control, one must take over the main power source, the electric. The truth is, a city can't run without a electricity, comfortably. He was trying to take away the rights of the Starmos citizens.Officer, I'd suggest you have this son-of-a-bitch arrested", answered Rubi.

"Was this his first offense?" asked the officer. The alien leader's wife hesitated.

"Eh. Uh. Um. Yes", she answered with a smile.

"Really, he's been arrested?" asked the general. "Eh. Wha. Um. Uh. Der. Yes", she answered once again with a smile, except this time around, her smile was wider.

"Why are you answering the questions

with hesitance?" asked the general.

"Because when I need to find an answer. It takes me a while. I know this man", answered Rubi.

"From what I see, this was a total mistake. He looks like he tripped into the lever, mistakenly pulled it, turned off the electricity, and caused this city to go into some chaos. I think you two should reconcile in front of me", replied General Valencia.

Rubi is looking up. The troops aren't able to hear her.

"It's good to be a liar. Lying is quite easy for me. Besides, I am quite good at making up stories and keeping them. Perhaps, I should make more stories up to keep up with my lying tactics. Sadly, I did not cause double jeopardy to Wilheim's life. Personally, I wanted him shot with those venomous, arsenic bullets. I wish that could've happened. One wouldn't know the burden being removed. This officer should be held accountable for harassing the hell out of me with asking ridiculous questions that are totally inconsequential for me to answer. Why of all things does he have to make me explain myself? If I don't want to explain myself, I don't have to. Wilheim deserves to die so that way he doesn't take the throne from my husband although he doesn't have any intent like this. I just want the throne so I can rule over Starmos. Wait. I am talking to myself", she said in an aside.

Fortunately, for her, neither the officers nor Wilheim heard her speaking. She lifted her head to get up from the choking and a large flat iron fell on top of her head. She is staring into space and fainted to the ground. Wilheim rolled out from underneath Rubi. General Valencia is laughing.

"What do you think of what's taking place right now?" he asked.

"She got what she deserved. She was this evil woman who did not care about anybody but herself and that's what happens to somebody that is evil. I would never think Rubi would have the capacity to be evil. However, apparently, my thoughts are false. She is genuinely evil", the alien leader's cousin answered.

"I don't think she's evil. She just made a mistake from what I've seen happened. She must've mistaken you for some sort of malicious intruder. I don't think you are evil. Rubi is too good to think of somebody like that. I believe she is too nice to be like that. It's not like she's so belligerent or bellicose with her attitude like you're making her out to be", replied the general.

"No, she can be very evil. I saw her lips moving in short asides. Unfortunately, I couldn't hear them because she was speaking through moving her lips. I couldn't tell what she was saying. Thus, I wouldn't be able to verify her comments. We all know she's very nasty. General, she's just putting on a show. She is being a facade. I've seen behaviors like that before. You're way too nice and too quick to give some folks clemency. You need to be a little bit tougher, especially on some folks like her. I think she's very arrogant with her attitude and self-centered. If you spent a whole hour with her, then you'd be able to understand", said Wilheim.

"I think you are completely making an exagarrent comment. I would not be able to concur with you on this. She seems less violent. She doesn't even seem volatile or have any proclivities to be volatile. Rubi, is a nice woman. Why don't you come to some sort of reconciliation with her?" asked General Valencia.

"How can you reconcile with somebody who admits that she is self-centered, takes one fake side of the law, and takes one real side of the law? You may be able to reconcile and empathize with some folks. Other folks you can't do anything about them. You can't negotiate with them. You can't speak with them. You can't even look at them in some cases. Rubi is one of the folks who you cannot negotiate with. She is somebody who will claim to reconcile with you and then she'll continue with some other violent action. That's just Rubi", answered the alien leader's cousin.

"I don't think that's true", replied the general.

"Now, let me tell you something. I guess it is important to reconcile with this woman. However, if she acts volatile or violent towards me ever again, you will be the one to blame because you were so loose on your policies with her. Instead of arresting her, you let her go free; but whatever. Let's reconcile so we are able to move on with our day", said the alien leader's cousin.

"Rubi, get up", said General Valencia. She is gradually waking up from her faint.

She is struggling to open her blackened eyes. Her eyes look like they have been punched through. Her face has scratch marks due to the strength of the metal. There are bruises over her head. On the top of her head, there are four welts. She is struggling to stand up and walk. Her speech is not impaired. She is limping to the alien leader's cousin.

"What do you want?" she asked.

"I want you and Mr. Von Alien to reconcile. I think you and him should both move on with the day because Wilheim acknowledged that you choked him by mistake. You didn't realize he was trying to fix the lever and he pulled it down by mistake. You thought he was trying to inflict harm against the citizens of the city. However, he was not doing such a thing. Although what you did was unacceptable behavior, I can concur where you made your move. So, you two shall reconcile", answered General Valencia.

Both apologized to each other in a phony manner. General Valencia and the troops marched out of the Secret Lair.

Chapter V: The Second Ordeal

The apologies finished and the general walked out of the room. The alien leader's wife and her cousin-in- law finished their ordeal.

"I am so angry at you. I should've killed you then and there like you deserved. You are somebody who's a meaningless creature. I knew you deliberately pulled that lever to call that damn Valencia in the room. Did you not do that? And why did you do that?" the alien leader's wife asked.

"You know what you are good at, Rubi?" asked Wilheim.

"No, please. I would strongly appreciate it if you would tell me what my specialty is", answered Rubi.

"You are very good at lying and making false allegations. You were the one who tricked me into thinking that this lever I can easily pull. Me, being the ignorant one, I pulled down the lever figuring not a single thing would take place or a good thing, rather. I didn't expect to be accused by you and I though this whole ordeal was over after Valencia was finished negotiating with both of us. Apparently, I was wrong about the definition of reconciliation. You need to be more respectful and kinder. You willingly apologized to me and willingly forgave me, not realizing you would pull such a deceitful and deceptive trick. Rubi, you are not the true one that I know. You are the woman who is violent and you are beast-like with your attitude", replied Wilheim.

The alien leader's wife's face is staring in shock. Her hand is covering her mouth and the parts of the eyebrows closest to her eyes are lowered and the parts of the eyebrows closest to her nose are raised. She is staring in utter shock. Her teeth are clenched in her mouth; but one cannot see it because her mouth is obscured by her hand.

She is looking at her cousin-in-law wide-eyed. She is not speaking in her natural voice. She increased the pitch of her voice.

"Wilheim, do you want to know about your true attitude?" she asked.

"Really? Is it that I am an honest fellow who is a gentleman and is nice to a nasty witch like you?" the alien leader's cousin asked in a smart aleck manner.

Rubi started to show her true anger toward Wilheim.

"Excuse me! What gives you the right to say this about me? What gives you the right to call me a nasty witch? Do you realize I was the one who put you on the list to enter where we are located? How can you act in the manner for which you are acting in? I will tell you what you are if you're willing to listen", she said.

The pitch of her voice decreased. At the same time, she was speaking in a hoarse, terse, and abrupt manner to him.

"Yes, please, tell me what you want to tell me. Be quite honest with me, for once. Don't be a sneak like you have been for a while, Rubi. Be quite frank with me. Don't distort the truth like you typically do. I believe you are good at distorting the truth, making lies, and being a huckster", said Wilheim.

"Alrighty, then, I will tell you what you are. You are a self-praising, arrogant egomaniac. You act in an audacious manner because you question my actions. Let me be very clear to you, what gives you the right to tell me how to behave and how not to behave? You are nothing but an idiot. You fall for all my tricks up my sleeve. You weren't the one who had to pull the lever. You chose to pull it. It's not like I've forced you to do that. Let me tell you that I don't force you to do anything. I don't force you to commit any crimes. I don't force you to call the military down here. That does not make me the liar. You are the fool, and you will always be one. You tout yourself to be intelligent and honest. Meanwhile, you are ignorant and gullible enough to fall for the trap. You've even admitted to being quite stupid", replied Rubi. "Well, I don't believe it was called for by tricking me. Those who trick are ruthless, callous, and do not have anything better to do with life other than to harm others. Why don't you perhaps learn to get a job, make something of yourself, instead of just sitting on a throne like the first lady would typically do! Perhaps, while you are sitting on that throne, you can contemplate your behvaior, and maybe you can learn a little more respect for some folks. I don't think your political position defines you. Rather, what defines you is your behavior. Your observable actions define who you are. Rubi, you need to learn to be a nicer woman. Maybe, you will learn if something bad happens to you. Your behavior is uncalled for and absolutely atrocious. I might be gullible but the phrase is this, 'too much laughter will cause too many tears.' What you find funny is joking at somebody's expense. Wait. You don't even find that to be funny. You actually bask in bad occurrences happening to some folks. Neither do I like anybody like you nor do I show respect for anybody like you. Rubi, your action to do this to me was inhuman. And that is the root of evil. You start off with doing small things. Then, you graduate to larger things. Before you know, it, trouble comes. In the dictionary, your face appears on the word, evil", said Wilheim.

"Okay, this bickering back-and-forth must stop. I think it's quite ridiculous and pathetic we are bickering over such a frivolous issue. Yes, it is my mistake. My actions were uncalled for. I should've never tricked you; but hey, you were gullible. I had to do such a thing in revenge for what you did to me. Let's just come to a negotiation and move on with our time here in the Secret Lair of the estate. Life needs to move on", replied the alien leader's wife.

"I think it would be fine to reconcile. We need to move on in order for me to get to tell you what's about to happen to Will. I don't think we are safe over here. I think Kerilic is still watching us. I am coming off that he is evil. I think he belonged to that damn SSGM Army. Now, I don't know if this is true; but from the way Kerilic is acting, he does belong to that volatile, beastly, cold-hearted, sinister, malicious army. Now, with regards to you, I will apologize to you for being so accusatory and confrontational with you. I think it's stupid that I am being confrontational. I will begin to atone for my behavior as you did. Instead of thinking, you were being nasty to me by making me pull the lever, there's a sixth sense that kicks in. This sense is rationale and thought on both sides of the fence. I only thought in my own sense. Now, I am thinking about my behavior in your sense. When you told me to pull that lever, maybe there was some sort of significance. There might've been some sort of lesson you were trying to teach me. And that was not to be gullible. So, you were extremely generous to go out of your way to place your hand over one word. Although I cost some folks their energy for a few minutes, I did learn a valuable lesson. Not only did you teach me that, but also, how to be aware of the surroundings. You taught me to be careful when somebody was telling me to do something. You taught me self-defense. I should've fought you when you lunged at me for my stupidity. You were right. I should've been arrested by the general. If I would've gotten arrested, then maybe, I would've been taught a valuable lesson. So, while I loathe your action and I forgive you for lunging at me. At the same time, I understand why you did that action. You had a couple of goals in mind to try to make me more alert of things taking place in my environment. Rubi, you are a good woman. You taught me very well", said the alien leader's cousin.

"Neither did you have to be so forgiving nor did you have to be overly self-critical. Just be Wilheim Von Alien. However, don't be a fool. Be an alert individual. I know you're a good man and you will always be a good man", replied the alien leader's wife.

"Thank you very much. Like I said, you were right earlier. And I should've been more conscientious", said Wilheim.

Rubi snickered.

"This is great. It is good to be a liar. I am good at reconciling with him. I didn't mean to tell him what I've just told him just about a second ago. He kind of deserves to be insulted. If he's going to be an idiot, let him be an idiot. Besides, I gain advantage out of that. I won't tell you the advantage I am going to gain because I don't want him to possibly hear me; but I am going to try to manipulate him so he can be killed. All he has been was a hindrance. He was the one that fell down because he was about to be shot by those Blanco Brothers. Personally, I would want the Blanco Brothers to kill him because he likes Will. I do want a failure near my husband. Failures are to be welcomed in this estate. I don't care what the Starmos folks think. I think it was necessary for me to be friends with the Blanco Brothers because they are definitely out to help kill my husband with their draconian attitude. Imagine me being the greatest figure in Starmos City. Wilheim, unfortunately, is going to stand in my way of being the next leader of this city because my idiotic husband is going to place Wilheim in his future seat for candidacy as President, once my husband's agenda is finished. Of course, I want my husband's agenda to be fulfilled. To destroy his agenda, I must attack Wilheim. I want somebody who is married to a successful Von Alien to take the power of future Leader of Starmos City. Wilheim, unfortunately, is going to stand in the way. I reconciled with him to shut him up because I knew he was going to cause trouble with me. The citizens will vote for Wilheim over me because Wilheim was a direct fighter for justice. To tell you the truth, I wasn't. I was just somebody who stood along side my husband the whole time. The only reason why I married my husband was to get the possibility of entering office. I have bigger plans than that. Wait, and you'll see", she said in an aside.

She walked up to the alien leader's cousin.

"Okay, let's move on. We need to head down to the train area. If you want to see more of the Secret Lair, then you will be able to head on board the train. First, we need to hit my fingerprint on the sign over here", she then said.

"Very well, then. We shall move along. The deal is this, though. If Kerilic had me removed from the list to go in the Secret Lair, then what would I do to gain access? I might have to go back and then I wouldn't be able to tell you the secret. That would be detrimental. I don't think you want such a detriment to happen. Do you?" asked Wilheim.

"Absolutely not. I think you're making me out to be evil. And let me assure you that I am not evil. I am somebody who is here to do good for Starmos City. In spite of me being the first lady, I will ensure that this city and all the best interests of the citizens are protected. I want to be able to maintain respect and I shall maintain it. We Von Aliens believe in a progression of this city", answered Rubi.

"Yeah, of course you believe in that", the alien leader's cousin said in a sarcastic manner.

"Are you being sarcastic and disrespectful towards me?" asked the alien leader's wife.

"No, I would never be sarcastic to you", answered Wilheim.

"Very well then. We shall carry on", replied Rubi.

Wilheim and Rubi are continuing to walk. They are walking side by side. The floors are changing from metallic to polished concrete. The lights are hanging two feet from the ceiling. They look similar to lights that belong in a gymnasium. The alien leader's cousin and Rubi have to be extra careful because their tall height will cause them to hit their heads on the hanging lights.

They are ducking constantly. The lights are hanging only four feet above the floor. Wilheim smashed his head on the last light. He became unconscious. He is having a temporarily retrospective blackout.

This blackout is showing a vivid recollection of his past. The first part of the blackout is showing his first year walking with his parents, who were following Cornelius in the creation of Starmos City.

Followed by that, he's recalling he being present at Cornelius's Royal Court at twenty and his parents being sentenced to life in the hole without parole for being accused of questioning the old brute's ideologies. The third part of the blackout shows him recalling the life in the tunnels. The fourth part is showing the time when the Blanco Brothers threatened him.

After, this unconscious, retrospective blackout, he awakened hearing, "Wilheim, Wilheim, Wilheim! You better wake up, now."

"Who are you?" he asked.

He's slowly opening his eye. He is struggling to open it. Rubi's face appeared right in front of him.

"Oh, it's you, Rubi", he said.

She pulled him up from the floor. He is feeling exraordinarily unaware of his surrounding. He is still partially in his unconscious, retrospective blackout. Eventually, he finally stood up from the floor after thirty seconds and became fully conscious.

"Wilheim, thank God, you are awake. What happened to you? Did you just faint out of the blue?" the alien leader's wife asked.

"No, I didn't. I woke up. I am sorry. I was just in a little trance. Wait. I just remembered, I hit a light", he answered.

All of a sudden, a blinking handprint projection appeared on the wall. This handprint appearance is light blue. This handprint looks like a grid. There are interconnecting lines making up this handprint projection. Rubi placed her hand right in the center of the projection. All of a sudden a luminous gold light is submerging from the ceiling. The lights in the hallway dimmed as this light came down from the ceiling.

"What are you folks doing?" asked the light.

"Who are you?" asked Rubi.

"It is I, Enkel, why don't you remember me? I am here to help you", answered the light.

"I don't remember you", replied the alien leader's wife.

She is looking at the angel with a sense of skepticism.

"Do you not remember me? I was with you back in the 1860s. I was with you when you were in Buck's abode. I was handling a luminous light", said Enkel.

"Where do you come from?" asked Rubi.

"I come from Starmos City. No, wait. You forgot where I came from?" asked the angel.

"Oh, yes. Now, I remember you. You were that occult thing. You were the one who was like a pixie. You had supernatural effects. You were the one who was following me to rescue my husband. That reminds me, I have to thank you", the alien leader's wife answered.

"Yes, about that. We need to discuss..", the angel was interrupted.

"What do we need to discuss, Enkel? I think I have a pretty good chance of going up to Heaven. I believe. I think I have a 80-100% chance of going up to Heaven and meeting the creator", said Rubi.

"Yeah, about that. You better stop your actions against Will. I know exactly your plan", replied the angel.

"What do you mean you know my plan? I am not planning to do any harm to Will at all. I love my husband", the alien leader's wife argued.

"Don't you dare take that tone with me, young lady. You need to possess some more respect. You don't disrespect somebody from up there like that. I mean it. You better be kind to me, I swear", said Enkel.

"What is your point of being here? To be another one who wants to be accusatory and belligerent?" asked Rubi. "I am not being accusatory at all. I am just saying", the alien leader's wife interrupted Enkel a second time.

"What are you accusing me of? There must be something that you have to say. Everybody's got an opinion. If you think taking Wilheim in this Secret Lair is wrong, you must be completely mistaken. I am taking him here to speak about a secret that he needs to tell me and it's regarding my husband."

"I am only here to give you good advice. Remember, man has free will. I'd suggest you'd turn back and tell Will the secret yourself. There'll be hell to pay if you go into this lair", said the angel.

"Listen up. I know exactly what I am doing. I am here to do good. So, don't tell me not to go in the lair. If I want to go in the lair, I can. If there's a secret that can harm Will, you are making the situation worse. This behavior is pejorative. You are causing trouble. So, maybe instead of making your little proverbs. Perhaps, you should keep your mouth shut", replied Rubi.

"Okay, what you sew, it shall come back to haunt you. There's a phrase that is often repeated that you might or might not want to hear. It's called, 'always let your conscious be your guide.' Apparently, either you are not using your conscious or you do not have a conscious. You might either be insensitive or evil. Rubi, you do whatever you want. It's your right. You have free will just like everybody else. I'd suggest you'd shut your mouth. I am going to go now. I can see your definitely not a believer in doing good. Therefore, I shall come back up to the ceiling and back up to the clouds. So, I shall hereby make a farewell. Just remember one thing. Not too many folks are able to see an angel like me. There are very few who an see me", said Enkel.

He returned back up to the ceiling. He is slowly returning up to Heaven. Eventually, he returned. All of a sudden, a demon with black wings is flying up from the ground. She is evil. She is dressed in the same sinister scarlet dress, last year.

Rubi came across her, a while back. Her lips are black. Her hair is black. She is wearing makeup that makes her skin look pure and perfect. She is evil. This woman came from Skull Castle, a while back. She has the sinister voice. She is very soft spoken, but extremely dangerous. She becomes angry when her agenda was never fulfilled. She popped on Rubi's left shoulder. She walked up to the alien leader's wife's neck. She kicked her.

"What are you doing here?" asked Rubi.

"It is I. Do you not remember me?" asked Jacqueline.

"No, who are you?" the alien leader's wife asked.

"It is I, Jacqueline Langyaw. I was the one who caused terror into your life. I was the one who inflicted harm to Will. I was the one who was Cornelius's fiancée. How can you not remember me? I was the one who supported causing harm. I was the one who told King Haggoth to come to Starmos City and bring back the tyranny. I was the one who supported evil", answered the demon.

"Now, what do you want you malicious beast?" asked Rubi.

"Why are you calling me a malicious beast? You were the one who rejected the angel. Damn that Enkel! You were the one who supported him being punished. And now you don't like me. What kind of woman are you?" asked the demon.

"I am a woman who defends her city because I am afraid the city is going to be returned back into a dictatorship if fools like you try and cause a large amount of harm. You are sinister. You are evil and somebody like you should be punished", answered Rubi.

"Well, I want you to listen to me because you've obviously rejected the angel. I am You will listen to me because I have to tell you something important. Rubi, you are nothing but a volatile individual. That's what your true conscious is telling you. The only thing that I can concur with on the angel is that one should always let his or her conscious be the guide. Your conscious was always meant to be evil. I know what you're thinking inside. You want to kill Will. You want him to be deceased. I know your motives. Why can't you just admit that to me? Be open about it. Don't be afraid to be prosecuted because you'll get off easy in this city. Hey, I did something evil. I supported a mass kidnapping and harm infliction to the citizens of Starmos City. In your mind and heart, you know you're going to get away with it. That's at least on your first offense. Hey, I got away with working as an accomplice with Cornelius by pleading my way out of the situation. I just simply had to give up my prosecutorial license. That's not a big deal. Besides, working on the show set was not a big pay. And I can tell you the prosecutor's office gave me end's meet salary. So, I had my heart set on being evil. I was born evil and I died evil. Nobody knows that I am alive; but I am planning to come back from the dead. And there'll be hell to pay. Do you want to help me fulfill my agenda?" asked Jacqueline.

"No, but I know where you're coming from. I want the same thing to happen to him", answered the alien leader's wife.

"Let me indoctrinate you with this, Will is a tyrant. He's here to cause harm. He's going to reverse the Cornelius way. Cornelius was great", said the demon.

"Yes, you're right except for the part about Cornelius. He was evil", replied Rubi.

"I can't concur with you on that one. However, I can concur with you on the statement that you were saying about taking back leadership. All you have to do is get Will. Make sure this plan works", said the Jacqueline.

"That's great. I think we should go through on it", replied Rubi.

"Good. I am going to be stuck in the chamber but, in case you need me. You can go contact me", said the demon.

The evil beast disappeared. Jacqueline is the representation of the devil, which speaks volumes of her prior behavior, while she was alive. Enkel and Jacqueline were psychological representations of consciousness in Rubi's mind. To the outsider, the conversation looked like Rubi was speaking to herself.

"Who were you speaking with?" asked the alien leader's cousin.

"Nobody. I wasn't speaking to anybody", answered the alien leader's wife.

"Are you sure you weren't speaking to anybody?" asked Wilheim.

"I was not speaking to anybody", answered Rubi.

"Prove it to me. The proof that I know to show you were speaking with somebody was that you were speaking in the form of a conversation. Being that nobody was in the room, you must've been speaking to somebody or you must have some sort of difference", answered the alien leader's cousin.

"Like I made clear earlier, I was not speaking to any individual. What the hell is wrong with you? If I was speaking to somebody, I would address that somebody by name. I did not speak to anybody else other than you within the past five minutes", answered Rubi.

"Are you sure about this because I heard some conversations? If you weren't speaking to anybody, then who were you speaking with?" asked Wilheim.

"I was speaking with myself. I was talking to myself", answered the alien leader's wife.

"Those who talk to themselves are not usually making conversations with themselves unless it is in dual role play in a theatrical event. We're not obviously in a theatre. So, may I please have knowledge as to who or whom you were speaking to? I think it's quite important if you ask me", replied the alien leader's cousin.

"Like, I said. I was speaking to myself. I think I am allowed to have some sort of a self-conversation. Besides, doesn't everyone talk to himself or herself at one point or another in his or her life?" asked Rubi. "Yes, folks do talk to themselves at different points in their life. However, they don't have self-conversations. That's not normal. I want to know who you were speaking with. It's important that you tell me", answered Wilheim.

"Like told you earlier, does it really matter who I was speaking with? If I was conversing by myself, I can. It's not your right to judge me. That's what I don't get in this World and this dimension. Why do so many folks have to be so judgmental?" asked the alien leader's wife.

"Yes, it is true that some folks are judgmental. At the same time, some individuals do things to evoke opinion. You, like most others, that including myself, are provocateurs. We all spark opinion and emotion. Rubi, you made me feel concerned that you were speaking with yourself especially in a conversational sense", answered the alien leader's cousin.

"I am being dead honest with you. I think it is fine for one to speak to himself or herself. It doesn't really matter. What matters is your opinion because if my husband Will, finds out that you believe that I speak with myself, he will have me detained for disrespect towards the leader and toss me out of the estate. And I don't want such a thing to happen. I want to be able to just live my life in comfortable peace, in a worry-free life. I guess that's not going to be the case because I have to be wary of all the actions that I take, the way I behave, and most of all, whatever words leave my mouth. Those are things I have to do as First Lady Of Starmos City", replied the alien leader's wife.

She finished speaking. She placed her hand on the projection print to gain access to the train. The hand print machine is processing. After three minutes, the alien leader's wife started showing a face of disgust. She rolled her eyes and is looking at the machine.

"What's going on with this? This annoying nonsense is taking place. I, so, hate the technology that exists today. I'd regret saying this, but some items from the Stone Age are better than some of the newest items here in this estate. I don't want to say I'd wish I'd lived in the Stone Age, but I am sure it would be much more relaxing to live in such a peaceful, nonchalant time period. Rather, than living in the time period right now: the impatient, pathetic, ridiculous time period. I mean, how can this technology get any worse, Wilheim?" she asked.

"Do you want me to be a smart ass who took what you said just literally? Or, do you want me to be honest with you regarding the complaint you have?" asked the alien leader's cousin.

"I think I will stick to both choices", answered Rubi.

"So, here's the deal. What happened earlier about the technology, I think it can get worse. By the way, this is the smart aleck answer. It can get worse because those who program the technology that we handle can use it to their advantage. They sell the technology in order to make a profit and then they keep realizing they can make the profit off cheap labor. This so that way you, the consumer, can be made to look stupid. Most consumer are in rushes. Therefore, they can't retrieve items that are considered flawed or breakable. On the other hand there are a couple of good sides to items being flawed. First, one is able to say that he or she, at least, tried the product and claimed disapproval of it. Second, if technology becomes worse, we might be able to speak with each other and keep each other comfortably at the dinner table instead of having our headphones on When you said, sometimes I'd wish we'd be back in the Stone Age, you bring up some pretty good but pretty bad points. There are a few good points. First, going back to Stone Age technology means the man or woman has to work. And I mean work. Second, going back to the Stone Age technology will increase familial communications and help bring families to be close knit. We, unfortunately do not see too many of those today. The Stone Age increased communication because it brought some folks together, and back then, individuals had to work as partners and help one another. Nowadays, everybody thinks he or she is so self-sufficient, and in order to get jobs done, nobody experiments. There's not any such thing as trial-and- error because in this society, today, one will feel alienated and there will be self-belittlement if he or she experiences a failure. Along with the good things of the Stone Age, there were some bad things. First, communication was precluded while being taken advantage of according to the means. One could not communicate with somebody from Garden City while being in Starmos City. No computers, no televisions, no radios, no nothing was around back then. The second negative aspect about living in the Stone Age was that one would not be able to live a comfortable lifestyle. In other words, one would not be able to even have something as simple as a light. Back then, lights were considered to show wealth. The third negative aspect about living in the Stone Age was that one was not able to own a business comfortably was because there wasn't such thing as trade or entrepreneurship. Not any individual had any money back then. Therefore, there wouldn't be any trade system. In the Stone Age, hunters and gatherers, particularly nomads retrieved food. Where did they have the time to trade or in some cases, make a barter? The exact answer is they never even had an opportunity to make a barter because of the hectic parts of their lives. Now like in every period, especially the Paleolithic and Neolithic Periods, there are good things and bad things. I think it is important to focus on the good things while we're alive. The only way we can die is if we become excessively poisoned or if somebody shoots us with a ray gun and kills us", said Wilheim.

"Are you done?" the alien leader's wife asked.

"Why would you be asking me such a ridiculous question? You know its not my cup-of-coffee when one asks me such an absurd question? That was you just now. Not only was I not done, but also, I was going to tell you something else that you should perhaps heed, Rubi", answered the alien leader's cousin.

"And what would that be?" asked Rubi.

"I answered your question regarding what's so great 'bout the technology in this present time period. However, you didn't answer my question", answered Wilheim. "What was your question?" asked Rubi. "How can you not remember the question that I've asked? How can you not remember the conversation we had earlier? Rubi, what kind of a woman are you?" asked the alien leader's cousin.

"What kind of a man are you to speak to me with such utter disrespect? This is stupid behavior. It's actually comical. You think I have this amnesia when I clearly do not have it. Your attitude about me is absurd. Why do you think I am somebody who is contemptible and disrespectable? Are you a man? A real man?" asked the alien leader's wife.

"Well, why are you giving me such a confrontation over a minute issue? I want to know who you were speaking with and why you were speaking with those individuals", answered Wilheim.

"Nope, you've got your answer wrong. Now, I can own you! Ha", replied Rubi.

"Oh, really? What does it mean to own somebody like me?" asked the alien leader's cousin.

"You don't know what it means to own somebody. I'll tell you what it means. Shame on you! Let me tell you something. What gives you the right to question my memory when you've forgotten the question you were supposed to ask me? You think you have knowledge about everyone and everything. You act like a news reporter or a paparazzi when you are nothing but a little nuisance. I know the question you've asked earlier, you've asked who I was speaking with, not why I was speaking to that individual. And yes, in an answer to your question, I was not speaking in a conversation to myself. I was speaking to two other fellows. Either you weren't able to hear them or you didn't even listen to the conversation being that it was a soft one. I was speaking with Jacqueline Langyaw and Enkel. So, can I ask you this? Are you finally happy that I've told you the answers you've wanted to hear? Are you pleased finally being able to receive some answers supposedly for once in your life?" asked the alien leader's wife.

"There's not any necessary reason for you to be such a smart ass with me. And besides. I didn't know you were able to speak with the dead. Do you have some occult powers that I should perhaps have some awareness of?" asked the alien leader's cousin.

"I do not have any occult powers. Once in a while, this happens to everybody. An angel and demon pops into the area for where you are presently located. I've met Enkel when he was an angel. However, I've met Jacqueline when she was actually alive. She was the devil back then. And she's still the devil, now. The only difference is that she is not in the physical presence unless one thinks about her or unless something happens where the devil calls up an evil creature. This creature usually shows some sort of deception. Both Enkel and Jacqueline come in the forms of pixies. The only differences are that Enkel is an angel and Jacqueline is a demon", answered Rubi.

"Now, were you the one who called Enkel down from Heaven and Jacqueline up from the Underworld?" asked Wilheim.

"None of your business", answered the alien leader's wife.

"What do you mean by which you have said, 'none of my business'? Did you call them both from the places of their meaning, yes or no?" asked the alien leader's cousin.

"No, I did not. Enkel came down voluntarily from Heaven to make some sort of conversation with me because he felt like having some company and Jacqueline decided to pop into the picture. I would certainly never call anybody down from the reaches of the underworld, Hell", answered Rubi.

"I don't believe you. You are..", the alien leader's wife interrupted Wilheim's statement.

"And why not? Is it cause you are the relentless cousin-in-law I have? Is it because you are the one who has been known as the failure?

Are you trying to insinuate that I call the demons to come up to the surroundings for which I am present in? Is that what you want to hear? Are you looking for some crazy answer you relentless, pest-like, bastardly insect?" the alien leader's wife asked showing a large amount of disgust.

She clenched her teeth on the last question she asked her cousin-in-law. A sigh of exasperation left her mouth after she asked the question.

"What is the deal? I think I know you have something to hide. Why weren't you speaking for such long intervals of time? Why did you feel guilty about answering my questions that I've asked regarding the conversation with the angel and the demon? Why did you call me those nasty, disrespectful names?" asked Wilheim.

"You're not insinuating that I am friends with the demon? Are you?" asked the alien leader's wife.

"No. Absolutely not. I am not insinuating you are friends with any demon whatsoever. I think, personally, you are friends with the angel. Not. The reason why I don't think you're friends with the angel is because somebody who's friends with the angel does not have anything to hide unless he or she is in kahutz with causing trouble with the angel. And

I don't believe angels cause trouble. Angels are good individuals. Angels do not have any problems with answering questions. You do. So, there must be some proof you have some relationship with the demon", argued Wilheim.

"I do not have any relationship with any demon whatsoever. If I was friends with a demon, would you think I'd be Will's wife? Would you think I'd be alive? I don't think so buddy. I wouldn't be alive because Will was the one who fought the battle against tyranny. He led the fight for justice. So, don't try and insinuate that I have some sort of camaraderie with Jacqueline. I do, however, have a small camaraderie with Enkel because he was the one that partially guided us when it came to fighting Jacqueline and Haggoth. He was the one who helped us. Don't be so accusatory. Your audacious behavior is not necessary. You think you are entitled to being so accusatory when I was the one who put you on the list to be allowed access into this lair. Let me tell you that entitlements are not allowed in this estate or in this city. You weren't the one who fought for freedom. And the freedom for most of the folks in this city did not come on any silver platter. For you, it did. I can see that through your absurd behavior", Rubi rebutted.

"Your statement about not having a camaraderie with Jacqueline is refuted because you stated, 'you want to make sure your words do not incriminate yourself for any reason.'

Incriminate yourself to what, Rubi? Incriminate yourself to committing a crime against Will? Are you planning something? I bet you know the Blanco Brothers and I bet you like them. Don't try and hide from the truth because the truth shall stand out against you. The truth will destroy your career and your life if it leaks", argued the alien leader's cousin.

"The truth. The truth. Maybe, your truth about me. The truth, in your eyes, is your assumptions about me. I have absolutely nothing to hide from anybody. I did nothing to nobody. So, why are you framing me with those accusations? Is there something you possibly have against me? Maybe, you're the one who's out to inflict harm against my husband. Maybe, you want to have the throne of Starmos City. Maybe, because you won your freedoms on a silver platter means that you want to deprive the citizens of their freedoms. I am starting to know the real Wilheim. And the real Wilheim is the Von Alien who I don't like. You are probably out to kill me", shouted Rubi.

"Oh, you are on the wrong side of the tracks, my friend, or should I say, my fiend. You are the one who has those ideas about taking over the Office of President of Starmos City. You are the one who has the idea of killing Will. The guilt is showing. A thought where 'everybody's out to get me' is a self- persecution complex. This is the one you have", replied Wilheim.

"You know something. I don't think this is worth fighting over this. We are arguing frivolously. The reason why I granted you access to this secret lair was because of a secret you were going to tell me. And it was a pretty important secret that you didn't want anybody upstairs in the estate to know. You were the one who wanted to be as far in the chamber as possible. Let's come to a second reconciliation, and let's agree to disagree about this allegation. I believe I am not out to get Will and I know that. You might think differently about my idea about Will. You can keep your truth. Let's move on", said the alien leader's wife. "I can truce with you, but I cannot concur with you about your thoughts about Will. I still suspect you're out to get Will", replied the alien leader's cousin.

"Whatever", said Rubi.

She placed her hand on the projection access entry. Then, she placed her eyes over the ocular lens. The ocular lens look like the inside of sun glasses mounted to a wall. She and Wilheim were given access into the third area.

Chapter VI: The Train Station

It is now half past nine in the evening. The alien leader's wife and her cousin-in-law are unable to tell time being that they are in an area without any clocks or without windows. This area has very Old World but New World architecture inside the station. The paints on the walls of station have a retrospective appearance, and the platforms are very unique. This is one of the very few operating, unoccupied train stations in existence.

From, the ceiling to the floor, this train station has unique architecture. On the ceiling, there are four domes. Each has a different painting within. The first dome depicts a graffitied portrayal of Cornelius leading the first generation of citizens heading to Starmos City. This portrayal is a vivid portrayal showing the orange mountains and the citizens throwing the cubes on the floor to make the buildings emerge from the ground.

On the right of Cornelius, Will was held in his parents' arms as an infant. His parents were standing next to Cornelius at the time, not knowing that they were going to be killed five years from that discovery date, March 21, 2020. None of the citizens, during that time, never thought he'd be a tyrant. They thought they would have a better life in this city. The tyranny of Cornelius and the brutality of his regime took over.

Then, the next dome depicts a stain glass mosaic of Will Von Alien. The hair looks inaccurate because it looks light blonde instead of dirty blonde. The skin is a tad darker than the real Will. This artwork depicts Will in a suit and tie representing his leadership of Starmos City. Adjacent to this dome, is a dome of significance. This dome portrays the colors of the Starmos Flag.

There are thirteen green lines and twelve yellow lines signifying the years Starmos City has been in existence. The green represents the openness for a better economy of this city. The yellow represents the honor and bravery for the ones who fought in the revolution against tyranny. The fourth dome is located adjacent to this dome.

This dome shows a portrayal of Will, Rubi, and Light on top of a plateau holding swords. Below the plateau, in the picture, are Cornelius, Jacqueline, Howard, and Mitchell rotting in a ball of fire. This is the most significant depiction in this train station.

This was a history changing event for a transition from Starmos City turning from a tyranny to a democratic government. This portrayal also serves as a lesson to make clear that evil never wins. Supporting the domes, is a multi-step ceiling. The steps of this ceiling rise up. The highest point in the ceiling is actually above the dome, that point being fifty feet above the ground.

The ceiling has a very rugged appearance. The reason why it has this particular appearance is because of the long history Starmos City has and the massive bumps in the road to signify the history of this city. The train station is formed in an A-Shape.

The North Wall and South Wall slant inward. The North Wall has a rugged appearance. There are large dome like windows push inward. The North Wall has a white color. This is the only part of the train station structure that is made of stone.

The dome shaped windows are also significant because they have a happy attitude in spite of the tumultuous history of the alien city. The North Wall is made of marble. This particular wall slants eight feet inward. The South Wall on the opposite side has a completely different appearance. Due to a superstition that walls facing South cannot be straight, this wall is curved when connected to the East and West Walls.

The superstition is that being that Jacqueline lived in a dimension south of Starmos City, she might return from the dead and cause a large amount of harm against the citizens of this city. This wall is made of stone blocks. The material is significant because it is made of sheer strength. This wall shows strength because it is pushed to destroy the evils of Jacqueline. In the center of this wall is a depiction of a skull covered by the Starmos City flag.

This depiction was to represent the evils of Skull Castle, and the Starmos Flag shows the victory against Jacqueline. In the station, there are twenty arches. Each arch stands at different arches. There are two rows of ten arches on each row. The North Row signifies the arches of Justice. Each arch has a significance. The first arch on the North Row stands at five feet in height. This arch shows the removal of Cornelius.

This arch has a blue color. The blue on this particular arch signify the hope for peace in Starmos City. The next arch depicts a sword, which is significant in freeing the citizens of California County. This arch stands at six feet in height. The third arch depicts words in Roman Font. The words shown state, "In order to have peace, there sometimes has to be war." These words are significant because Will had to shoot the guards who were protecting Cornelius and Jacqueline.

Then, the fourth arch stands at ten feet in height. This arch is made of shining gold. The gold represents justice in Starmos City. The gold is the color of a typical justice scale. This arch signifies the Trial of Cornelius. The fifth arch depicts the verdict of the trial. The worlds of the verdict are engraved in the granite arch. "When there's guilty, for the evil ones, there's justice. The sixth arch depicts shells engraved. These shells signify a hopeful future of Starmos.

The seventh arch, eighth, and ninth arches are made of black, white, and grey marble. These arches show the differences of the justice system. The black marble, grey marble, and white marble arches stand from left to right. The black marble arch is on the left.

This arch signifies the old tyrannical justice system under the reign of Cornelius. The second grey arch located in the middle signifies the transition of the justice system from a tyrannical one to a fair one. The white arch on the right signifies the honor, dignity, and respectability of the new Starmos Justice System, where fair trials take place and evilness is eradicated.

The last arch is made of rugged curves. The rugged curves signify a judge's white robe. The last four arches described stand at a staggering twenty feet in height. The South Row of arches signify the new Starmos City government.

All of these arches are made of white marble. The white marble signifies purity of the city. There's only one arch, which is made of black and white marble. That arch being the one in the center. The smallest arch stands at a small ten feet in height. This arch represents the Election of Starmos City taking place for ten hours. The adjacent arch stands at twelve feet in height. This arch represents the Balance of Power of Starmos City.

In the center of this particular arch is a justice balance. The adjacent arch stands at fifteen feet in height. This arch represents the power of righteousness. This righteousness arch features a four feet in height by one foot in width Cross. The fourth arch stands at seventeen feet in height representing a negative occurrence.

This arch does not have any engraving. This arch signifies the story of Will being part of the estate under the Tyranny of Cornelius. The fifth arch is the tallest arch at the train station. This arch stands at forty five feet in height. This arch stands above the track. This arch is made of black and white marble stone. The black marble stone is featured on the right side and the white marble stone is featured on the left side. The white marble stone represents the hospitality of the citizens welcoming the foreigners, the black part of the stone. This arch is also significant in showing that Starmos City is divided but united.

In spite of there being a variety of ethnicities, this arch is to show the universality of the city. There's also a third significance of this arch. This arch shows the different political parties in the city all fighting for the same cause, that cause being the justice and freedom for their constituents. The sixth arch represents Peace. This arch has a curved appearance because Peace is never rugged. Peace is pure. Therefore, the curved appearance represents purity and the rugged appearance represents evilness and harm.

This particular arch stands at eighteen feet in height. The seventh arch stands at twenty five feet in height. This particular arch represents the Age of Will when he gained control over the alien city. The eigth arch has gold and emerald painted marble. These colors a significance because they are the same colors as the Starmos Flag. This eighth arch stands at twenty feet in height. The ninth and tenth arches represent the heights of the alien leader and his wife, Rubi. The ninth arch stands at six feet in height, which represents the height of Will.

And the tenth arch stands at five and eight-tenths of an inch in foot height representing the height of Rubi. While the train station has Old World and New World architecture, the train in this station is not your typical train. Although the train is not present at the train station, it does function on a track; but not a typical track. The track looks like a massive slab of concrete. Within that concrete, are magnets.

There are about ten magnet at this station. Each of these magnets weighs one hundred pounds. The function of the magnets is to serve as a power booster for the train. The magnets are moved by a machine to be having forced polar energy. The forced polar energy launches the train at light speed. One would not be able to see the magnets in the concrete track. The concrete in the track looks rugged and hard. However, it is hollow.

The alien leader's wife and her cousin-in-law, Wilheim, walked on the platform. There's a yellow and black striped line in front of the loading dock for the train. Very few individuals have ever passed through the doors of this Secret Lair to the train station.

"This is impressive and significant", said Wilheim.

"I know. I see it every day. It's just one of those mundane things that one sees on a daily basis", replied Rubi.

"Really? You actually see this place on a daily basis?" asked the alien leader's cousin.

"No, I was just trying to make you feel enchanted with my life. I think you'll be able to enjoy this platform", answered the alien leader's wife.

"Well, that was not really necessary. Are we going to be visiting some place nice so I can tell my secret to you?" asked Wilheim.

"Oh, yes, we are visiting a nice place", the alien leader's wife answered in a sarcastic manner. She scoffed bluntly and smirked after she made that comment.

"You know. The time is coming. It is coming closer to time where this man is going to meet his fate. I am sorry that I was being so dismissive in my interview with this man; but when one is trying to accuse me of something that is horrific, I am going to get extremely defensive, especially in cases of crimes like murder in the first degree. Yes, I was speaking with Jacqueline. I called her up from the Underworld to Starmos City. My intent is to cause harm. I am still not going to reveal my plans because I don't want anybody to know. I will make this point to you. Something good during the day is not going to happen. It is going to be an extremely tragic day, and there will be trouble today. There will be tumult today. There will be danger today. There will be danger for my husband for Wilheim, and for the citizens of Starmos City. This day will be a tough day. There will be a horrific event ending in a tragedy. There will be hell to pay, today. Wilheim will wane away when we will win. I will be joining the coalition with Jacqueline to bring back Starmos City. I will make sure she is able to come back from the dead. She will no longer be dead when I take leadership. Starmos City will be under my control after Will leaves office. And this transition will be a very peaceful transition. Whereas, neither Will nor Wilheim be allowed in this dimension. They will be eradicated from the dimension for good. We will make sure they don't come back. If they come back, they shall be killed. I don't care what the court of public opinion wants to say about me. The citizens will be able to complain all they want; but when Will goes, the citizens will be complaining themselves to the jailhouse and the poorhouse. It will be their problem. After all, they were the cause of their own problems. I wasn't. This is during the time I become leader. If I don't win, I am screwed. I don't care; I just want my husband out of here once and for all. We Von Aliens do not have any justice due to Will being the leader. Besides, he is not a true Von Alien. He doesn't have that true Von Alien self-righteous, self-praising, ridicule citizens demeanor about him. He is too nice to the citizens of this city. And they don't deserve somebody to treat them nicely. Look at what the citizens encouraged. They encouraged him to commit the wicked crimes. The citizens were the ones saying the 'three cheer's' for the death of Jacqueline. They were having a massive party when Cornelius was killed celebrating victory over Starmos City. What victory, may I ask? Victory for Will? That's not victory. That's just causing trouble. The justice system was good when Cornelius was leader having just one procedure where the criminal wouldn't be put to trouble. The leadership was good under Cornelius when the city was controlled by the police and citizens didn't have much to say back then. Television was more entertaining when Jacqueline was on the air. She was tough, and we need somebody like her, not somebody who's weak. We want justice. We citizens want fairness. I meant I want the Cornelius leadership to be running the city. It will be great. Goodbye, Will, leave this city", Rubi said in an aside.

She laughed in a diabolical and sinister manner after she said this aside.

"Rubi, what are you doing? And can you give me the reason why you were just laughing in such a devious and evil manner?" asked Wilheim.

"I'll answer the first question to you; but I won't answer the second one", answered the alien leader's wife.

"Why can you answer the first and not the second?" asked the alien leader's cousin.

"Because I can answer the first, but I would not be able to have any for the second", answered Rubi.

"If you can answer one question for me, but you cannot answer another question. There's something wrong with you. I am going to order you to answer both questions, and I mean it. You better answer both questions that I ask you", said Wilheim.

"You don't tell me to answer any questions. I won't listen to your secret. I will make sure you are expelled from that list, and I mean it. I don't play any games. I am very serious when I make a statement. It is not your right to tell me what to do", Rubi replied in a brusque manner.

She bluntly continued laughing diabolically.

"There must be something for you to hide. You are laughing in such a diabolical manner. Your intent is to cause harm. Rubi, you are nothing but a malevolent beast. Now, answer the two questions", argued Wilheim.

"Fine, I will answer. The only reason why I am answering is to shut you up. I was laughing because I saw something funny on my phone, and that is just my natural laugh. That's an answer to the second question, Mr. Technical. The reason why I was staring at the wall for a long period of time was to find the button to call the train down here so you can be safe. I don't want anything to happen to you. I want your secret to be safe and addressed properly. It would be a major flaw on my part if I did not have your secret addressed. So, I hope you are happy that you have the answers to the two questions that came out of your mouth. It was quite necessary that you asked me those wonderful questions", Rubi said in a sarcastic and deceitful manner.

When she gave the answers, she was lying through her teeth. Not a bit of the truth came out of her mouth. The only part of the statement that she made that would be considered as the truth was when she wanted Wilheim to shut up. She does not have a clean conscience, for it is poisoned with the chemicals of evil and malice. Wilheim completely disregarded Rubi's sarcasm and utter disrespect in the comment she previously made.

"What are you doing now? Sending the train down here?" he asked.

"Honey, I would love to tell you that right now. And I am doing that. The train is going to be here in about thirty seconds to five minutes. I am here to help you, Wilheim. I am trying to get the train to come down here as fast as possible so you can tell me the secret. I know you are waiting to extract that out of your mouth, and I know you're waiting to spill it. So, you will be able to do such a thing in a few minutes. Honey, just hold on for a few. I am sending the train down here in an answer to your question", she answered.

She is speaking in a smart aleck manner, which is very disrespectable and dishonorable. Her mouth can never be loathed enough for it sounds like it has been bitten by a viper. Her attitude is evil and sour. She doesn't want to reveal the truth about herself. She is speaking to Wilheim like he is uneducated and does not have one bit of intellect.

"I don't get it. A few minutes ago, when both of us were in the hallway, you were extremely nasty and dismissive to me. Now, you're being extremely nice to me. What's the issue about that? You are now so quick to call me 'honey.' I bet you don't even call your husband that. That is too nice of you. In fact, it is odd of you to do such a thing. Don't ever call me that again", replied the alien leader's cousin.

"You are my honey. I will call you honey as much as I want. It is my prerogative. It is my special right to call anybody any name I want to call them. So, if I want to call you honey, I can. Let me tell you something. I do not have multiple personalities. This is my genuine personality; but I do have a multitude of emotions. When one gets me angry, he or she will feel my wrath. When one gets me happy, he or she will feel my love, for you in the past ten minutes made yourself feel my love. You deserve it. You are a great man, Wilheim. Don't make yourself a bad one", Rubi lied once again.

She hit the red button to call the tram down here.

"Whatever. You are who you are, Rubi.

There's nothing I can do to change you. You are very disrespectable, though", replied Wilheim. "I am not asking you to change me. I am who I am. Accept me for who I am, for I am here to bring goodness to you. I am a great woman. I am somebody that's here to bring great love in this World and make the aura a positive one", said the alien leader's wife.

She gave a sinister smirk and a disdainful appearance to the alien leader's cousin. She pressed the button to send the train. Enkel has emerged from the ceiling and came down to Wilheim's shoulder.

"Wilheim, I want to tell you that there are some issues around here. I am sure you find something quite fishy and odd about the way Rubi is behaving. If you think she is being genuinely nice, that is not the case. She is an evil wench. Rubi is out to cause trouble. Although she claims she is not here to get her husband and you, she is lying to you. She is planning to kill you, and when she does that, she won't feel any remorse. I mean it. Rubi is an evil individual. She is malevolent. She is like a fiery, fierce serpent, who is out to inflict harm and danger. Do you want to go to the rest of the Secret Lair with her?" he asked. "I don't believe you for one second. I do believe in you and worship you. However, you are not somebody to tell me that Rubi is out to cause harm. She is a danger and her motive is to be malevolent. Her soul is filled with malice. Maybe, you'll eventually understand when something happens to you. I am warning you, she is of great harm and she will strike whenever nothing goes her way. She is spoiled ever since she has been the leader's wife. She is out to kill Will. You might not realize that, but that is true. Can't you understand her evil demeanor? Can't you understand her bitter attitude? A bitter individual would not show you anger in front of you. A bitter individual is here to inflict harm. And a bitter individual will not show that he or she is here to inflict harm. That individual will hide behind a curtain to protect himself or herself from being implicated to harm others. She is hiding behind a curtain. Can't you notice in her attitude?" asked the angel.

"No, I don't see one bit of evil in her. Like I made clear to you earlier, she is not here to cause any harm. She is not here to cause any harm. I don't see her as that. I am sorry I'm not believing you; but this is something where I cannot concur with you on. Rubi is too nice. From what I've heard in the past, she lived a pretty rough life. There's not any way where she can be considered to be a spoiled princess. She is not even a princess. She is a first lady. She might sit as a figurehead. She is not the woman you're portraying her to be. I'd recommend you'd keep your mouth shut about Rubi. She is nothing you portray her to be", replied

the alien leader's cousin.

"Whatever. At this point, I give up. You win, Wilheim. Your behavior is fine. What ever happens to you, I am not going to be there for you. What you sew, you shall reap, for you have not listened to me. I will not come back unless you beg and plead for me to come back. Is that understood?" asked Enkel.

"Yes, sir", answered Wilheim.

Enkel returned back to the Celestial City. The alien leader's cousin and Rubi are waiting for the train to arrive at the station. They are sitting on benches and elevator music is playing. Harpsichords started playing in the background. It is now ten in the evening. A zooming noise is being heard. The train is moving at light speed. WHOOSH.The sound of the train makes. ERRR! The train made an abrupt stoop at the station.

"Welcome, train", said the audio on board the train.

"This goes quite fast", said Wilheim.

"I know. It moves at light speed", replied Rubi.

The train is a black car. There's a tinted window. It has the similar curved shape of an LSC, but it doesn't have the same wheels as an LSC has. Instead, there aren't any wheels on board this train. The train is supported by magnets, which propel the train to move at extreme speeds. The train moves at mach one thousand speed. The train is comprised of one car.

The train has a trunk, which holds the emergency engine. This engine has several pipes. The engine helps the train move quite quickly during an emergency. It charges when traveling on the track. The train has a lift side door. One would just simply hit a remote control to initiate the door's movement. The door takes approximately twenty seconds to open and five seconds to close.

Therefore, one has to enter the train as soon as the door rises up. The train has two flame design side stickers. This side stickers were designed and printed by a compute, and they are just simple magnets. Fortunately, these magnets do not interfere with the train's movement. The train has emergency wheels, which serve as automatic breaks if the train is moving at dangerously high speeds.

Also, when the magnets are not working, the train drops on the track and the wheels emerge from the train. They, the wheels, touch the track in an emergency. The demon, Jacqueline, emerged onto Rubi's shoulder.

"What are you doing here? What the hell do you want?" the alien leader's wife asked.

"Are you kidding me speaking in such a disrespectful manner? I have a great idea for you. I'll help you fulfill your agenda", answered the demon.

"You'll help me fulfill my agenda?" asked Rubi.

"Yes, I will help you fulfill your agenda", answered Jacqueline.

"What exactly are you going to do to help me fulfill my agenda?" asked the alien leader's wife.

"Here's what you will do. First, you are to be deceptive to Wilheim.

"Politely, act in a welcoming manner and make sure he boards the train. Make him feel comfortable and be extremely kind to him. At the same time, don't be too kind. The reason why is because Wilheim will suspect you're up to something suspicious and you will be sceptible to accusations, and you saw how the drama was like earlier today with those damn inquiries that Wilheim was planning. After you trick him, after boarding the train, you will jump on top of the train. When you do that, you will hold on real tight because you might be dead. So, take the chance. Then, you will succeed by making sure he's dead. If he dies, then your agenda will be fulfilled, sort of. Now, the third thing you'll do is that you will secretly follow him to Elitrionic Mask. He and Elitrionic Mask will have a long discussion, and the mask will give him instructions on where to go. From there, the mask will ask you what your purpose of being in that dimension. Then, you will tell him that you don't have time to talk. He's usually very vulnerable. After that, you will follow Wilheim around the dimension where he's not supposed to be and you will kill him right at the perfect moment. In order to keep your plan covert, you must do a few things. First, keep your voice in the form of a church mouse. Do not make any noise whatsoever. That's the last thing you want to happen. Noise is the ultimate harm. Making noise will be a deleterious move, which can definitely destroy your plan and agenda. The second thing you must do is that you must lie and remember those lies. If you lie to somebody, you better keep that lie to yourself and never talk to that individual ever again, even if it's your own husband. Thirdly, make sure you do not make any change involuntarily or deliberately. Whatever you do, don't change your plan. Changing the plans can cause a possibly detrimental effect in your agenda and your life might be destroyed. Fourthly, you better psychologically rehearse your answers. An important thing you must do is not show any rehearsing of answers to Wilheim. He has an inquisitive and intuitive mind where he can find out easily what you do. So, in case anybody asks you questions, rehearse your answers in your mind. Now, I want to ask you if you have any questions regarding the issues that's taking place", said Jacqueline, the demon.

"Now, if necessary, what would be the alternate plan? Now, I made clear, if necessary", asked Rubi.

Jacqueline is showing a large amount of fury because of the previous question. She impaled the pitchfork into Rubi's arm. Sharp searing pain has been felt in the alien leader's wife's arm.

She screamed. "What did you do that for?" she asked.

"Because you asked an absurd question. First, you are going to go through with my plan. If that doesn't work, then I will tell you about the alternate plan", answered the demon.

"No, tell me about..", the alien leader's wife was interrupted by Jacqueline.

"The Alternate Plan?"

"Yes, please tell me about the alt", answered Rubi.

"Fine, I will tell you about the alternate plan. Here's the deal. Well, we would have to have several different alternate and depending on the case by case scenario. If Wilheim does not enter the train, you will enter the train first. If he leaves you on the train, you are not to program the train to move on the track. And therefore, the only way the train will move is if he's forced on the train. Once you force him on the train, gag him, and bring him to the Evil Underworld Dimension. And that's where he'll die. I will kill him because in exchange for that, I will make sure you bring me back from the dead. Then, if the next part of the plan is foiled, this is what you'll do. That, being the part about making up the stories. If he finds out you are lying or if he even tries to insinuate that you are lying, then you are to kill him immediately or destroy his body to the point of death. Have him ran over by the train. I know what you're going to ask so I have the answer for the question, which you are about to ask, that being the stories you're going to tell. First, you will make up a story regarding that you've gotten lost in the Alien Estate and you were mistakenly taken to the dimension on the train down here. You will make up a story stating that Wilheim kidnapped you and brought you down here to make you die with the rest of us evil immortal souls. Then, the third story you will tell is that you have died and you have returned back from the dead because somebody exhumed your body and placed an occult effect on your body. That's what you're going to do to me when you enter the Underworld Dimension, you will have me exhumed. If that doesn't work, you will make up a hostage story. The hostage story you're going to make up is that the Ghost of Jacqueline held you hostage psychologically and you can't move. That will be a desperate end. If you're really desperate, then make up that you are mentally ill and you entered this area without rationale. When you meet, Elitrionic, you are to show him great honor and respect. In spite of him not being open about who enters and exits the Underworld Dimension, you are to be kind to him. He is going to be just as inquisitive and possibly annoying as Wilheim. This is the place, however, where you will be able to drop off Wilheim and have him removed from Starmos City, and he will be dead for sure like you want. The only issue is that Elitrionic is going to question you for the reason as to why you want to kill Wilheim. He is the man that you can actually be genuine to. You can tell him your agenda without being caught, and in exchange for my release and exhumation, I will have both the train's regular and emergency operations disabled to that way there's not any way, Wilheim will be able to return back to the city. I will make sure that you have your agenda fulfilled because somehow your agenda and my agenda are connected. If Elitrionic has a problem with you killing Wilheim, you will explain to him that Wilheim held you hostage and forced you to come over here. You will also fake in the train ride, that you gagged him to stop him from trying to kidnap you and hold you hostage. You will claim that he was going to kill you. Now, those are the alternate plans. In order to carry killing Wilheim out, you must have a few good qualities. First, you have to be an extremely good liar. You must stick to your story so not anybody finds out that you are lying. Second, do not leave any tracks. While you are committing the crimes, you are to wear rubber gloves to hide your DNA. Don't step in any dirt, and don't touch anything unless you have to. Thirdly, keep this adventure covert. This is not like chess where you can pull a gambit. You cannot sacrifice anything small for a larger gain. This plan has to be carried out so that way your agenda is fulfilled. Don't let anybody but myself or Elitrionic have any knowledge about your agenda. Fourthly, hide. Once you carry this plan out and Wilheim is dead, you are to leave Starmos City with not a trace. The reason why is because in spite of Officer Kerilic being on your side, there'll be somebody else who will take over his spot, and you don't want to go under investigation and possibly be castigated for such a horrific crime. Rubi, be very careful. Listen to me because I know how to carry out covert missions. Although I didn't get away with kidnapping over six hundred individuals, I did gain a victory and I did win the first leg of the war", said the demon.

"Jacqueline, I agree with you on everything except for one thing. You are not right on abandoning Starmos City. I don't want to leave this city because this is the place where I've been living. I don't want to leave. I want to stay. If I leave, I will be a vagabond and I will not know where to go or how to live a new lifestyle. I've already acquiesced to the lifestyle of the First Lady of Starmos City. You know what I will do as an alternative to the plan? I will stay at the Alien Estate and not let myself slip. I will keep the killing of Wilheim a dark secret from Will. If he asks where Wilheim was killed, I will lie to him and tell him that, 'I do not have any knowledge about the death of your cousin, Will.' I'll tell him that. Depending on if I feel he's about to find out, I will poison him. He won't know I am going to poison him because I will not make the poison seem obvious. I will lie to him and tell him that I have apples to bake, and I will make sure he is fed an apple, I mean Arsenic Pie for breakfast. That's how he'll die. He'll die the same way as his cousin, Cornelius died", replied the alien leader's wife.

"Good, that's an excellent alternative, which I've never contrived in my head. I guess that's what happens when you are convoluted in such an intricate plan. Before you officially go through, I want to make sure your plan is not truncated or discovered by those who should not have any awareness of the plan. The first piece of advice I must give you is to allow Wilheim to tell you the secret before you kill him. The second piece of advice that is a must that I shall give you is that you will have to be extremely covert when it comes to carry out the plan and don't let anybody, I mean anybody, stand in your way or investigate you. Kill that individual if he or she is going to question you and I mean it. You can't let anybody question your idea or try and stop you from carrying out your plan. Rubi, being that I gave you instructions, I think you have knowledge and clear awareness as to what you must do", replied Jacqueline.

"Yes, I think you are absolutely right. I do have a large amount of knowledge as to what to do and how I shall go through with my plan. Now, I will board the train, and I won't need you any more", said Rubi.

"I don't know 'bout that. You might need me at some point during this rigamarole because you might need me to help you fulfill your agenda", replied the alien leader's wife.

"I don't know about that", said the demon.

"I think I have knowledge as to what I am talking about. I will see you later. Wait. You will see me later", replied Rubi.

"No, it's actually. I will see you later because I am the one who's coming back from the dead because you're going to exhume me. Right?" asked the demon.

"I don't know about that. Maybe", answered Rubi.

"Why not? You sick, twisted, deceitful liar", asked Jacqueline.

"Because where you are located is the Underworld. There are usually evil things down there. I don't want to risk my life to let you out. I am only doing this because I want to rule Starmos City", answered the alien leader's wife.

"I will go away; but whatever you sew you will reap, and it'll come back to haunt you. You better have me exhumed somehow, someway, somewhere, and I mean it. I am being very serious and clear with you", replied the demon.

"I don't care. If I don't feel like having you exhumed. I don't have to have you exhumed. You will stay there for eternity, Jacqueline, because that's where you belong because you are evil", said Rubi.

"You are calling me, 'evil.' I am not evil. You're the one that's being evil. You want to kill Wilheim and your husband so you can take the leadership of Starmos City. And you want to rule the city similar to the way Cornelius ruled it", replied the demon.

"Yes, that's true. However, maybe you should learn to think before you speak being that you're the queen of deception. You need to stop looking at the splinter in my eye and you should look at the log in your own eye. You make me out to be this demon when you are clearly the demon. You are the one who kidnapped those 600+ individuals. You were the one who imprisoned the 150+ citizens of California County. You were the one who committed the most troubling crimes", said Rubi. "Whatever, you do whatever you want. The plan I told you, you better listen to it because it is something that will put you back on the right side of the tracks. If you are somebody that is true to your word and somebody that is fair with whatever you are doing, you will free me from this eternal, torturous prison. Rubi, I know the kind of woman you are. You are the one who is inconsistent, parasitic, and doesn't do any good deed in exchange for an action that you said you were going to do. Rubi, I know exactly who you are. Looking back, I should've never helped you on what you wanted. I should've never given you a plan to fulfill. Rubi, you are somebody that I don't like and all you're going to do is cause trouble. Rubi, you only do things for yourself. You don't do it for nobody else. You are a self-centered individual. Unlike you, I at least risked my life and died to try and fulfill Cornelius's agenda. There was only one part of my agenda and that was to arbitrarily prosecute the citizens of Starmos City and all of the political dissidents. And even that was to fulfill Cornelius's agenda. Rubi, I would hate to be someone like you because you are nothing but trouble", replied Jacqueline.

"Yes, whatever you say. I will fulfill the agenda against Wilheim. I don't know about Will. Will is my husband. Wilheim is just an annoyance. However, you don't have a bit of love in your heart. At least, I had some form of love until you came along and until Wilheim started annoying me. You were the one who poisoned me with this evilness and rancorous attitude", said the alien leader's wife.

"I shall fade away. You shall carry on. However, we shall eventually die. You might be in the same place that I am right now, that being the Underworld. If you don't go to the Underworld, if you change in any way, I shall go haunt Starmos City for eternity. And I mean it", said the demon.

She disappeared. Rubi turned on the button to open the door. She and Wilheim entered the train.

Chapter VII: The Secret Unveiled

It is now eleven in the evening. The alien leader's wife and Wilheim have just boarded the train. The train has a large control panel inside. The right side of the control panel serves as the general purpose for the movement. The orange button means for the train to reduce speed. The red button is used for an emergency stop. There's a large screen in the center of the right part of the control panel.

The screen has keyboard. The operator will type the name of the destination on the train. Once he or she hits the green button, the train will move at high speeds. Once the train is coming close to the station, he will let the driver know that it has arrived. The train features a video screen to show different movies at different times of the day, for which the train is moving at.

The train shapeshifts into a robot when there aren't any occupants on board. In order to be comfortable on the train, one can lay down on the black carpeting on board. The curved window is tinted. The train serves a dual purpose. It can work as a Light Speed Cycle.

The train's primary purpose is to serve as a robot and an LSC.

"Who enters the train?" asked the LSC.

"It is I, Rubi. Who are you?" asked the alien leader's wife.

"You don't remember who's on board the train? How can you not remember? Do you remember the one who drove you around different places and chauffeured you? Do you remember who's the commissioner of transportation appointed by your husband?" asked the LSC.

"Are you Light S. Cycle?" asked Rubi.

"No, really? Of course, I am. How come you don't remember me? Is it because you are the First Lady Of Starmos City? Do you think you have a special right to forget the folks who built you up?" asked Light.

"Of course, not. I am not the type to forget who my fellows are, especially the ones who constructed me and built up my life. Light, I am sorry for not realizing it's you. The thing is that I wouldn't know that you could run on a track. I thought you were just some sort of mundane train", answered the alien leader's wife. "Well, I do serve a trio of purposes. I become a life-size robot when I am around some folks. When I'm on the road, I become an LSC. When I am on the tracks, I turn into a train. My blue paint changes color when I turn into a train, it changes to a white color to integrate with the area. I camouflage with the area because when I am on this track I am not heading into a good area. I transport the guards to the Secret Lair to the Underworld to make sure the evil dead are staying on their eternal prison. Believe me, it's hell down there. Now, what's the reason why you are coming down here?" asked the LSC.

"Because I can", answered the alien leader's wife.

"What a stupid answer. I cannot accept that. There must be more to that answer than what you're telling me", argued Light.

"It's a must that I have a private discussion down here. Wilheim needs to talk to me about something. It is something that's very important, and I would like to keep what he's telling me in confidence", said Rubi.

"No, I won't go unless you have him tell me the secret. I will keep the secret he must tell me confidential", replied the LSC.

"Can both of you please? Light, I can't tell you the secret because you have too much contact with the outside World, and I don't want anything to happen just in case you slip with your mouth. I don't want to take that chance. Can you just go so I can tell Rubi the secret?"

asked Wilheim.

"What audacity! Young man, you have a lot to say for somebody that I didn't meet", answered Light. "Are you an LSC?" the alien leader's cousin asked with a sense of fascination.

"Yes, I am", the LSC answered in a nonchalant manner.

"Well, you are amazing; but I am not telling you the secret that I must tell Rubi. I hope you would not mind that. Would you?" asked Wilheim.

"Absolutely, not. I respect the fact that some things of yours need to be kept confidential. That's just on of them. Wilheim, I will drive you and Rubi to the stop where you need to go", answered Light.

"Hey, why do you think it's okay for him not to answer one of your questions, but it's not okay for me to answer one of your questions? Essentially, why do I have to explain myself and he doesn't have to explain himself?" asked the alien leader's wife.

"Because I know you, and this is my first time getting to know Wilheim. In fact, this is the first time I've met Wilheim. So, I am to be respectful. They say, 'sometimes your first impression is your last impression'. I like Wilheim", answered Light. "Well, that's very nice of you to say that, Light. That was an extraordinarily respectable comment", replied Wilheim.

"Don't mention it. Now, can I ask you this one question?" asked Light.

"What may you want to ask me?" asked the alien leader's cousin.

"Would you mind giving me a background about your life: where you came from, how old are you, your family, and your life in Starmos City?" asked the LSC.

"I wouldn't mind telling you such a thing. Let's start with my birth. I was raised in this city. Thirty years ago, I was with my parents Cornwall and Horace Von Alien. They were young parents, at the time. Both being twenty five years of age at the time of my birth. When Cornelius founded this city twenty five years ago, I was with my parents as a five year old. We originally came from Ford City, which was an interesting city, very similar to Starmos City, except it was older and developed by humans, and sold to aliens. Cornelius led a band of Ford City natives out of the city and brought them over to Starmos City, where they would develop the city by throwing blocks of pre-programmed buildings on the ground. From there, those buildings would pop up. Cornelius wanted to turn this city into a democratic republic, at least this is what we heard. However, he became too power hungry. One year after the creation of Starmos City, he turned the place into a socialist government. He started by taking over businesses. Then, he interfered with civic jobs like my father and Will's father. Then, he eventually started taking over lifestyles and daily life such as eradicating religion. Cornelius ran this city in a tyrannical manner. When he saw that there were dissidents ready to attack him or even when he suspected there would be dissidents, he would start committing mass persecutions. My parents were killed at the same time Will's parents were killed. Cornelius was nothing but a tyrant. And he destroyed my life. He caused people to die in a genocidal manner. Now, if I may tell you about how his tyranny affected my life, I will be glad to. When I was younger, I was growing up like any other youth attending Primary and Secondary Education. His tyranny did not cause an effect on those years. Rather, it caused a major effect on my Post-Secondary school years. When I was younger, I wanted to go to college but because Cornelius was evil, he was against college education. He overtaxed my parents to the point where we had to move out of our house and move to the church. His purpose in doing that was so that way we wouldn't be able to have an opportunity for me to attend college outside of this city. This was to cover up Cornelius's tyrannical regime. To add insult to injury, we got a memo from the Alien Estate. This memo stated that preachers were to quit their jobs, churches are to leave this city or be burnt, and religiously affiliated citizens must quit their religion or die. Cornelius was turning overly tyrannical. So, we moved down to the secret tunnels of Starmos City. The tunnels were nasty, disgusting, and we had to make sure that we would not constantly freeze. Fortunately, Starmos City was and still is uninhabitable for any animals like insects, rats, mice, or rodents in general. So, we were lucky for that being the case for us. My parents still had their jobs. My mom worked alongside Will's mom as the Comptroller for the City and my dad worked along side Will's dad as the one who managed the reservoir. However, when the reservoir closed and both our dads were fired, our mothers were the only source of income. Therefore, Cornelius accused our mothers of committing embezzlement in the first degree when they didn't do anything wrong. He upgraded the charges to treason and sedition and killed both our mothers and fathers. I was twenty at the time and Will was fifteen at the time. He kidnapped Will and pushed him into forced servitude at the estate. And I remained in hiding down at the church", answered the alien leader's cousin.

"Would you mind please telling me about your relationship with Cornelius and your relationship with Will? Are you a true Von Alien?" asked Light.

"Yes, I am. So, is Will. Our mothers are not. The lineage of the Von Alien Family traces back to the 1970s. In 1975, my great-grandmother, Martha, and my great grandfather, George Von Alien were born in Ford City under the human leadership. They died in the 2015 Storm. They were affluent and affable. I was told that they were wonderful to be around. They had a kid in 1995, Cornelius and Wilheim who married Wilhelmina in 2015. They had me in that year and Wilhelmina's sister married an unnamed Von Alien, who also lived in Ford City. Cornelius was born twenty five years before I was in 1995 to a non Von Alien. Then, Will came along. Cornelius founded Starmos City. The timeline of the existence of the Von Alien Family is confusing. So, I can't really explain it any further. The only ones living today are myself and Will. Everybody else either died off because they were executed by Cornelius or they died in the Storm of Ford City. I am thirty years old and I was born in the year 2017. Ford City is now gone in the wind because of the 2015 Storm. Folks stopped flocking there", answered Wilheim.

"That's pretty interesting. Are you a true Von Alien?" asked the LSC.

"I am not what you'd call a true Von Alien. Wait. Umm. Quite frankly, I don't really know. I would have to do further research and I don't have any time to do such a thing", answered the alien leader's cousin.

"Would you ever do such a thing given the opportunity?" asked Light.

"To be honest with you, if I had time, not really. I wouldn't do such a thing because I remembered some of my family members, who've adored me and I don't want to be shedding any tears because it would be traumatic for me to look back and remember my parents being shot under the despicable, evil tyrant, Cornelius. So, no, I wouldn't. I think my answer is pretty clear on that question", answered Wilheim.

"Well, can I ask you this important question? Did you ever plan or lead any revolution against Cornelius? Did you want to lead any revolutions against him? Did you every carry any of them out?" asked the LSC.

"To answer your first question, yes, you can ask those three questions. To answer your second question, I planned plenty of revolutions. The first one I've planned was a mass evacuation from the city having all new buildings programmed into boxes, and we would go to a different part of the desert to develop a new city. The second one I've planned was a mass rebellion and a destruction of all the buildings in the city including the Alien Estate. The third one I've planned was a mass raid against Cornelius. The fourth one I've planned was that we would not show up to work and sit around doing absolutely nothing all day, which would cause Cornelius to abdicate the throne. To answer your third question, no, I have never led any revolution against him. I've sought advice from my parents and some of the Von Aliens, they didn't want me to lead a revolution against him because of the detrimental consequences of being charged with sedition and the fact that the family would have been divided if Cornelius was to die or be overthrown. To answer your fourth question, I've never carried them out even without the advice of my parents. I thought to myself even further. My good conscience was saying not to overthrow the dictator. My true conscience was saying to be rid the city of tyranny. I listened to my good conscience because I didn't want to die by firing squad or even take any chance of dying by firing squad. Fortunately, for Will, he carried out the revolution against Cornelius very meticulously and strongly. On a daily basis, I psychologically and sometimes verbally commend his methodical and strong thinking when it came to dealing with this revolution and be ridding this city of all tyranny. And I bet you the citizens would thank him consistently. My cousin is an extraordinaire and I hope to be placed in an administrative position under his leadership. He's done a great job for the city, as he should and as he will", answered Wilheim.

"Yes, that's nice. Do you want to know some information about me?" asked Light.

"Well, being that I've never been in or even met an LSC, especially somebody with some personality like you have, I would love to know a lot of things about you", answered the alien leader's cousin.

"You think I am very fascinating?" asked the LSC. "Of course. A vehicle that can talk is always something intriguing to me. Please, go on and tell me about your life", answered Wilheim. "Well, what would you want to know? Do you need to ask me specific questions about my life?" asked Light.

"Well, yes. I am going to talk to you in a question by question basis. Let's start with the first question. Can you give me general story about your life?" asked Wilheim.

"I'd be delighted to. I had a pretty interesting life. I was born right here in the Starmos LSC Factory, the grey building, which was a factory. I am made of a lot of metals, which make me sun proof. I was a chauffeur for Cornelius. That's who I was meant to be with. I was meant to drive folks like him around. I also shape shift into a robot, and I have a big personality. I am practical and intelligent. I have a computer system built into me and video game system to entertain the folks who are on their way to head on long distance trips. I am about fifteen years of age; but I have the mind of an intelligent computer system. For a computer, I never go out-of-date. I am always upgrading myself and rebooting myself. I have been to many different places including some of the cities around the World. I've been to most of the dimensions. Of course, my home city is Starmos

City. I've traveled through time during the 1800s in the Civil War Period. I've been to New York the most amount of times. In addition, I have dual citizenship. I am a citizen of Starmos City and California County. I can travel at mach seven thousand mph. My life has been extremely interesting for the most part. At the same time, there were some stormy parts of my life", answered Light.

"Yes, those were general adventures. I want to know about a chronological order of your life. I want to know about your family, your friends, your favorite places, your favorite things to do, the interesting parts about your life, and the most crazy adventure you have ever taken. Can you please tell me about those things?" asked the alien leader's cousin.

"Well, I don't really have any parents. I was made from a computer in a factory. Do you realize that I am not a human or an alien? I am born in a factory. I do not have any parents. Therefore, I don't have any family. I do consider some folks to be like family. They're called great lifelong friends of mine. I am friends with your cousin, his wife, Officer Kerilic, Mayor Stone, Commissioner Clayton, Officer Johnstone, Tom Jackson, and Emperor Gairdon. Gairdon unfortunately died because of two psychopathic living allies of Jacqueline. If you want to know more about these folks, Mayor Stone, gave me carte blanche to move freely in California County, NY; Commissioner Clayton, was the police commissioner who helped me during my fight against Jacqueline; Tom Jackson, was a fool who entertained me and he helped me during my time in California County; Officer Keriilic, helped investigate the assasination against Gairdon; Gairdon, helped me rescue my friend Tom. Sadly, he died because of two sick bastards, who belonged to Jacqueline. The most favorite place that I've enjoyed was Garden City. Although my friend, Tom, was in a horrible situation over there, I must admit that Garden City was beautiful. I remembered the palace was a shining monolith. It was massive. When I arrived in the city, the palace shined in the sunlight all day. What I could never have forgotten was that the palace was made of sheer silver, gold, and bronze. This palace had talking flowers. In spite of all this opulence, the emperor was extremely respectable. He was extremely helpful and most of his constituents showed a great deal of honor towards him. The most crazy adventure I've ever had.. Hmm. Unfortunately, that was a traumatizing but relieving adventure. I remember the time. It was when Jacqueline Langyaw was in existence. The night of Cornelius's death and Starmos Independence Day Celebration, Jacqueline kidnapped me. She nabbed me in the sleep after burglarizing the Alien Estate and held me hostage. She forced me to fly her to the Skull Castle Dimension, where I was enslaved on her farm. I was forced to live here as a slave and do work twenty four hours. For seventy two hours, I was stuck here. Fortunately, Will and Rubi rescued me, and Jacqueline was killed. To see that Jacqueline was killed was relieving. The best part was that I brought Jacqueline right to the courthouse to face justice. She deserved the punishment. Even better, on that day, I saw Will shoot her. There was justice that day. I would say was probably one of the best days of my life", answered Light. "Good points. Can you tell me what you did in California County?" asked the alien leader's cousin. "I've been to California County twice. The first time was to speak with Mayor Bill Stone, who Tom told me about. The second, was to rescue all the townspeople of the the county from the brutal officers of Cornelius", answered the LSC.

"That's it? No, there's got to be more. Would you mind telling me about each experience in each individual entirety?" asked the alien leader's cousin.

"Sure. It was the summer of last year Will, Tom, and I were fugitives escaping Starmos City. That was when Jacqueline went on the air. And she found out our getaway spot, that spot being California County. Jacqueline and Cornelius led an army of evil aliens. Twenty four hours before they can reach the city, I alerted Mayor Bill Stone and told him to print out PSAs of the invasion. I had lunch with Mayor Stone and told him about what was taking place and telling him about Jacqueline's evil agenda. When we gave out the PSAs, we led an escape into the woods. I found the

Woodstons. They helped me discover Garden City with some supernatural map. The second time I visited California County was to rescue the citizens of the county and to prosecute Cornelius and Jacqueline. Jacqueline got away with the crimes because she pled guilty in exchange for testifying against Cornelius. Cornelius, was shot. Those two times were not interesting times. The county looks like a typical suburban area. The people there are kind of introverted and gave me an odd look because of my speed. So, yeah, those were the two times I've visited the county", answered Light. "Can you tell me about the time about Garden City? Can you tell me about some of the citizens there?" asked the alien leader's cousin.

"Absolutely. The citizens in this area were nice for the most part except for this group, the Spazerstocks. They were walking stick insects, who were spies for Cornelius. I wonder if they've ever been tried in Garden City for the crimes they've committed against the citizens of Starmos City. They were the ones who forced Tom to be with Monstre, a swamp monster who lived in the sewers of Garden City. However, they were very accommodating to us. In spite of them being vegans, they did serve delectable salads and we've escaped to Gairdon's Palace. We arrested the Spazerstocks and brought them to trial for kidnapping Tom. They faced execution because the cruel and aggravating circumstances of their crimes allowed them to have their charges upgraded to crimes against humanity, which is a capital offense. They have supposedly been sentenced to death. Yes, that was my experience in Garden City. I had some pretty interesting experiences in my life. I've traveled to lots of places, more places under Will's administration than Cornelius's administration. I was able to be free with Will being Leader of Starmos City and the revolution", answered the LSC.

"Those were quite unique experiences, especially about the one in Garden City. I wish I can visit the places you've been to. I can't wait to see Earth. That's going to be great. I do not just want to go to one county. I want to spend at least thirty days on Earth", answered Wilheim. "Very good. That's very nice. Now, instead of just sitting here all day like a bunch of spuds, we should talk about your destination as to where you are headed to. So, please, can you tell me where you are intending on going todday?" asked Light.

"We are heading to the Underworld. We have a special purpose of being there", answered the alien leader's wife.

"What would that purpose be?" asked Light.

"To speak with Jacqueline", answered Rubi.

"Do you really want to go there? You

may be sucked in there and never come out. Do you want such a horrible event to happen?" asked the LSC.

"I don't mind risking my life. I am all about taking risks. Please, send me down there, for I shall come back to you", answered Rubi.

"What about Wilheim? Is he coming with you?" asked Light.

"Of course he is. He's going to be the one who is going to protect me. He is going to be the man who is going to help me stay up strong in this World. He is going to be the one who is going to let me out and rescue me if anything happens to me", answered Rubi.

She snickered after she made this statement.

"My plan is coming close. The time is near. It is time to carry out the plan. I am going to deceive Light to show him that Wilheim must come with me when he honestly does not need to come with me. Light is going to be the one who will assist me in killing Wilheim, who deserves to die because he's been nothing but a hindrance to the mission. Jacqueline and I will have a victory in Starmos City. Don't mistake me for a fool. We will start and win the war against Will. We will turn the Alien Estate from an invincible mansion to a blaze. We will turn all the buildings in this city from towering monoliths to ruins. We will turn the citizens from once thriving individuals to either imprisoned or deceased individuals. We will kill every member of the government or indoctrinate them into going back to the old philosophy of Cornelius. Our agenda will work", the sinister alien leader's wife said in an aside.

"Wilheim, do you really want to go with Rubi?" asked Light.

"To be honest with you, no. I definitely do not want to go with her to this place. I am afraid of the perilous implications from visiting this place. I am afraid of dying. I am fearful of being imprisoned and tortured. This place is going to be a living hell", answered the alien leader's cousin.

"I am surprised at Rubi that she wants to free Jacqueline. She stood by with her husband for a while when there was a massive war against tyranny. Did she get poisoned by the power of the purse or the title? I hope she doesn't have anything against me. Or, does she?" asked the LSC.

"Now, these two answers are just speculation from me. I am pretty sure they're true; but don't depend on me being the sole individual to answer the questions. To answer your first question, I believe that it was both the power of the purse and the power of the title of first lady. The reason why I believe it's the power of the purse is because when some folks have a large amount of money and living in an affluent estate, then they become to power hungry. Sometimes they go as far as killing the folks in the household so that way their power can increase. The power of the name of first lady, I also believe, was a large contributor with regards to her attitude. Being that she has that name behind her, she thinks she can do whatever she wants, whenever she wants, and she wants to do it. She wants to kill Will and I because she wants her agenda to be fulfilled, that agenda being a revival of tyranny. She was only nice and she aligned herself with Will because she wanted to move into the estate and know the insides of the estate. This was so that way she can get her evil, despicable, disrespectable agenda fulfilled. She is not the woman you thought she was; that woman being a nice, innocent, kind, loving, benevolent, and affable woman. She is a snob and an evil, malicious, devious individual", answered Wilheim.

"In spite of making such a long statement and pushing to bring damning evidence to convict and punish her, I just cannot be swayed by your statements to lean on your side. I believe Rubi is a loving woman who shows a lot of courtship and honor towards her husband. I don't think she's a volatile woman. I don't think she's the picture that you are trying to portray her as. She is not malevolent. I just cannot believe a word you are saying", replied the LSC.

The sinister smirk on the alien leader's wife's face is starting to show. The four inch wide grin is starting the other show. A quiet, evil laugh left her mouth.

"You know something, Light. You are one hundred percent right. I am not evil. He's lying. He is making this all up. I was always out to help my husband and so was he. I am starting to question his ideology. Light, I am not this sinister malevolent woman like Wilheim is putting me out to be", she said.

"Good point, for the most part, that is. I don't see Wilheim as a liar. I believe he is a good individual like everyone else here. I don't think he's out to get Will. I don't think you are out to get Will. I do believe that you are a good woman. Can you please tell me what that snicker that just came out of your mouth was for? Please, can you give me the significance of that snicker?" asked the LSC.

"Light, Light, Light, I am not the woman you think I am. I am not this evil individual who is out to cause harm and eradicate lives. I am not a power-hungry individual who craves power simply because I have a large purse. I am not an individual who is here to cause harm as the First Lady of Starmos City. I am not a husband killer. I am not a gold digger. I am not a supporter of Jacqueline's Way. I am somebody that is a fighter for justice. I just have the wrong way of coming off. I am an innocent woman being framed by this low life next to me", she lied through her teeth when she made this statement.

She said this previous statement in such a melancholy and pleading manner to the point where she managed to gain Light's sympathy.

"Oh, my dear Rubi, I feel extremely bad for you. How can folks batter you in such a manner? How can Wilheim accuse you like this? We live in such a terribly accusatory dimension", said Light.

In spite of his computer programmed intellect, he is gullible enough to be tricked to Rubi's deceitfully, deceptively, sinister moves.

"I was just lying through my teeth as I said this. Wilheim is right. I am a criminal. I do want Jacqueline's Way to dominate this city. I do want Will dead I do want Starmos City to go downhill. Am I a fighter for justice? Puh. No, I am not the fighter of the universal form of justice. I am a fighter of my justice. I am a fighter of my beliefs. I just like to keep them in secrecy. I have been doing a very good job of keeping my ideologies in secrecy, for the most part, that is", the alien leader's wife said in an aside.

"Light, it is hard for to understand why you are defending this woman. Do you not realize she is lying? I am not making false accusations. If you notice why she doesn't talk that much, she is contemplating plans to cause trouble", said the alien leader's cousin.

"You know something. I will take your word. I am sorry that I was kowtowing to her beliefs. I am just plain gullible to anybody. I notice she's not talking that much, which can be a possibility. Now, in order to keep your mouth shut and her mouth shut, I will stay with you when you meet Elitrionic. This is in case anything happens to you. If anything happens to you and she kidnaps you, I will follow you to the Underworld Dimension. This is so that way I am a witness and I can have General Valencia lead the Starmos Military into the area. Hopefully, not anything will happen to you; but in case anything does, you will be safe and there'll be a witness to say that you were abducted in that particular dimension. To satisfy Rubi, I will drop you off at the dimension. I need to satisfy both parties because neither you nor Rubi are causing me to take any sides. Rubi and yourself did not cause me to take any sides. Therefore, I shall remain neutral and satisfy both parties. I will drop the two of you off in front of Elitrionic. We will handle the issue from there; for now we are to try and remain quiet for the rest of the ride", replied the LSC.

He is trying to mitigate the situation. Rubi knows she is devious and evil. She is deceptive and sinister with deceiving Light. She is underhanded and sly with her movements.

Wilheim is trying to tell the truth and persuade Light. Rubi is trying to keep her cold-blooded, evil attitude under wraps. Light is just trying to keep the peace and prevent any tumultuous situation from taking place.

"When are we going to get moving?" the alien leader's wife asked in an impatient manner.

"Now", answered Light.

He departed from the train station from zero miles per hour to one thousand. He is moving at extremely high speeds. He is increasing the speeds as he travels further onto the magnetic track. It is now five seconds post departure.

"How fast can you possibly go?" asked Rubi.

"How fast do you want me to go?" asked Light.

"As fast as you can", answered the alien leader's wife.

"Are you sure? Because you told me earlier, you want the window to be rolled up. Is that correct?" asked the LSC.

"I've never said any such thing. However, now that you mention it, I do want the window rolled up", answered Rubi.

"Are you sure about that and traveling at Mach 7000?" asked Light.

"Yes, I am positive", answered the alien leader's wife.

He rolled up the window and started increasing his speed. Five seconds into the ride five hundred mph. Ten seconds into the ride one thousand m.p.h. The rate started doubling. Wilheim and Rubi were pushed up against their seats. Their mouths are widening, their eyes, tearing, and the wind of the speed of Light being felt across their faces. Their skins are extremely sensitive to the wind.

Neither are the two in pain nor can they communicate if they were to be in pain. One minute into the ride with Light traveling at mach five thousand mph.

"You two seem quite quiet back there. Do you need me to slow down? Do you need any medical assistance? Are the two of you alive right now?" he asked.

"Slow down", the two answered in a murmur. Light cannot understand what they are saying.

"What? What did you say?" he asked.

The two raised their voices and tried to articulate their words better. They repeated their previous statement verbatim except louder. Light still wasn't able to understand. He repeated his previous question verbatim. They kicked him. He felt pain and slowed down.

"Now, this is what happens when you kick me. Are you two selfish or what? What's the deal ? Why did you two kick me?" he asked.

"Because my evil, I meant loving, self felt like doing such a thing", the alien leader's wife answered sarcastically.

"Don't listen to her. Her statements are a bunch of hogwash. The reason why I kicked you and probably her is because we needed to get your attention. Because we couldn't clearly and eloquently articulate our words, we had to get your attention. So, we kicked you", answered Wilheim.

"That's a good reason. I am sorry for slowing down. Do you want me to..", Light was interrupted by the alien leader's cousin.

"No! Don't speed up! Do you realize that we can possibly get killed. Do you realize that we can miss the station? Do you realize that I feel extremely uncomfortable back here?" asked the alien leader's cousin.

"Fine, I won't raise the speed. I will close down the window if you want. Besides, we are right near the station. I wouldn't want us to miss the Underworld Station, which is the terminus station for the train. I am sorry that I've made you feel uncomfortable back there", said Light.

"Although it's not fine that you've made me feel uncomfortable, it is fine that you've apologized to me. You're forgiven. Can you give us the ETA?" asked Wilheim.

"About thirty seconds to another minute", answered Light. "That was pretty quick", replied the alien leader's cousin.

"Yes, sir", said the LSC.

"You know something, Light. I am a little bit angry at you. You pull this kind of..", Light interrupted Rubi's statement.

"You told me that I pulled a kind of what? Did I pull a shenanigan? Did I do anything to wrong you? Did I do anything to make you unhappy?" the LSC asked in a sarcastic manner.

"Excuse me! Did you just speak to me with such an utterly disrespectful tone?" asked Rubi.

"No, I just spoke to you the way you speak with everyone else, a demeaning, disrespectful, phony, and sarcastic tone. So, I decided to give you a taste of your own medicine", answered Light.

"He just owned you on that one. You better watch what you say", said Wilheim.

"You, shut up", the alien leader's wife replied.

"Light, you can let us off over here", she then said.

"No, you let me fulfill my duty of driving you to the Underworld. I am sorry to tell you the truth; but that's just plain ol' protocol", answered the LSC.

"Yes, I don't care about your protocol rhetoric. There are two ways you get things done when I'm around. It's either my way, where things will be handled peacefully, or the highway, where things can get pretty ugly if you know what I mean. It's your choice. Chose to stay on my good side and there won't be any tumult. Go on my bad side, then there'll be a ton of tumult", replied Rubi.

"Excuse me. Although you are the first lady, or at least you think you are, you are now inside of me. You are in my vehicle. You will keep your mouth shut, and you will listen to me. You don't have any right to behave the way you are acting. In fact, I see the real Rubi. I see the real you. You are nothing but a sinister low life. You are a peril to society. You are a danger.

And you shall be ashamed of yourself based on your attitude. Please, I want Wilheim to tell you the secret. I want to hear the great secret that is hidden. I want the connection to be seen. I want to see what your ultimate agenda is, Rubi. I've heard it through the grapevine about your agenda. I've heard it all over the place. These rumors may still be rumors. However, they might be true. Rubi, what are you? A monster?" asked Light.

"You do not have any proof to back up the details about your case. I cannot believe what you are saying. There's not any proof to verify or substantiate what you are saying. You are totally wrong. You are an evil LSC. You are here to cause trouble. I can't wait to walk outside of you, and I don't want to see you ever again infinitely. If Will needs transportation, he is not going to use you, he is going to use the train. We don't need you that much, even though you're more direct. So, let me be clear with you, you are causing nothing but trouble. Don't try to be a wise guy. Don't make up lies. Don't look at me. Neither do I want to see you again nor do I want to see Wilheim again. Will sure as hell doesn't want to see you again", answered the alien leader's cousin.

"Rubi, you keep saying the bull crap rhetoric that's coming out of your mouth. It is nothing but stupidity. You are an insolent idiot. Your behavior is not just any idiosyncracy. Rather, your behavior is a danger to our society.

Your behavior is who you are. I know you don't like to face the truth; but you are evil. When you stay quiet for those long periods of time deliberately, there must be some suspicious behavior", replied Light.

"Your behavior is disdainful and is the epitome of accusatory behavior. There are some folks who are just plain quiet. You are the ignorant fool, who is quick to aggravate the hell out of me. You are the one who is annoying and ridiculous. Your behavior is so absurd, it's not even funny. It is very asinine. So, maybe, you should perhaps learn to keep your know-it-all mouth shut", argued Rubi. "Don't you dare take that tone with me, young lady! I have been on this planet much longer than you have. Now, you are about to leave me. Hopefully, you will change your behavior after you leave the Underworld, that is contingent if you make it out of the Underworld", rebutted Light.

He moved past the flash of light, headed into the Underworld Dimension, and arrived at the station. Rubi and her cousin- in- law departed the LSC.

"What's the secret that you must tell?" asked Rubi.

"Yes, Wilheim, what's the secret you must tell us?" asked the LSC.

The alien leader's cousin is turning red

and his skin is sweating. He is sweating to the point of a florid appearance.

"Spill it, Wilheim", said the alien leader's wife.

"The Blanco Brothers are going to kill Will. They are planning to maliciously paralyze him. They are going to destroy him and the whole estate", cried Wilheim.

He almost bursted into tears.

"Oh, wow", the alien leader's wife said and then chuckled.

"You sinister, despicable individual. How can you do such a thing? How can you react to such an imminent threat and laugh with regards to your husband's life being at stake, never mind your husband the one who founded this city. You are a beast. I now have knowledge about the real Rubi", said Light.

"That's one thing that you were right on, for once in all the time that I've known you. I was evil all along. I was just acting like a fighter and being with Will to take the throne of the First Lady of Starmos City. Did you think for one second I was trying to help Will? I was only doing that to gain power? I am the one who was being the huckster the whole time. I was the one who was here to cause trouble. I have been secretly friendly with Jacqueline. Sadly, she's dead but I am going to rescue her", said the alien leader's wife.

Chapter VIII: Elitrionic Mask

Light remained at the station so that trouble would not ensue in the Underworld. The train station of the Underworld has an opulent appearance. The ceilings of the train station are supported by three hundred stone arches. The layers of stone are three feet thick. The alien leader's wife and Wilheim walked up to a massive stone wall with two ten feet tall wooden doors.

Featured on the doors, are massive gold knockers, which have an appearance of a lion's face. The gold knockers are about two feet in height and one foot in width. Supernatural effects are about to take place. The gold knockers have a sinister facial appearance. The lion knocker on the right is Leonard and the lion knocker on the left is Leo. Leo has the more combative and brusque attitude, while Leonard has a more nonchalant and calm attitude.

Leo is very abrupt and blunt with his manner. Meanwhile, Leonard is very smooth with his manner. Leo always has his eyebrows lowered. Leonard has his eyebrows at a normal level. The gold on Leo is rusted due to age. The gold on Leonard is shining due to his youth. Leo has a chip on his forehead; but Leonard has an immaculate appearance.

Leonard shines in the white stone and fire. On the other hand there's not any effect to Leo because he has an extremely dusty head. Leonard is constantly ecstatic and healthy; but Leo is very drowsy, weak, and angry. Leo uses his energy to make folks happy. Leonard uses his energy to be a guard. Leonard has reverence and shows honor towards Leo because of his venerable age. Leo believes that Leonard is this ignorant and pathetic youth, who shouldn't be in existence. Leo believes in supporting wars and violence.

He basks in bad things happening to others and in some cases, he thinks it's funny. Leonard believes in keeping peace and he feels mortified when one dies or when a war takes place. Leo honors the empress. Leonard despises the empress; but doesn't show it. Leo believes Leonard is a traitor. Leonard believes he is just speaking his mind. Leo believes that Leonard should not be a door knocker because he believes that Leonard does not have respect for authority.

Leonard believes that Leo is a citizen who shows honor towards the Underworld and he (Leonarrd) is trying to model his behavior after Leo's, alluding to the loyalty of the Underworld. Leo, although he believes that some folks should not be using him as a knocker because of the age and comfort of being a knocker, he has acquiesced to being one. Leonard dreads those using him as a knocker and he bites the individual's hand whoever is using him. Leo does not believe in belaboring his work or having a conversation with the guests who enter the Underworld. Leonard is very quick to make conversation with some folks who enter the Underworld to try to get to know him better. Leo, believes in causing supernatural and dangerous effects to take place.

Leonard believes in not pranking the ones who visit the Underworld. Leo supports keeping the ones who visit the Underworld there forever so not anybody who decides to leave can use the left door to leave. In spite of Leonard not being used as a knocker, he does not mind when some folks use him as a door, contingent on if they don't slam it. Leo does not sing. Leonard does sing, his singing voice does not sound melifluous.

Leo does not support modern technology such as LSCs and automatic doors. Leonard does believe in honoring technology and respecting the value of it. Although Leonard does feel inclined to let outsiders into the Underworld, he does not let his guard down. If he feels there is some suspicious activity taking place or if he feels there's a suspicious individual entering the Underworld, he will stop that individual from entering. At the same tie, although Leo believes in not letting any outsiders in the Underworld, he does believe in letting some outsiders in based on credentials and prior behavior outside from visiting the Underworld. Leonard was shipped to the Underworld from Earth.

Leo was naturally born here. This speaks volumes as to why his attitude places a negative aura in the environment, for which he's located in. Additionally, he believes that not any single soul should be questioning his ideology. On the other hand Leonard is fine with folks asking questions. Three-fourths of the time,

Leonard shows a smile on his place, which gives a welcoming, hospitable appeal to outsiders. Leo always has an angry face. His teeth are showing to the point where they sometimes freeze, and a maintenance employee would have to place olive oil and vinegar in his mouth, which tremendously burns his mouth. Since he is made of gold, one would not be able to see the burn marks. Leonard has the capacity to move his ears and eyes.

Leo does not have that capacity because he is an older door knocker and he shows a negative, stone, cold face attitude and expression. Leonard is friendly with Elitrionic. Leo does respect Elitrionic. However, he's not most friendly with him. Leonard once had the capacity to walk because he was once a living Lion Statue on Earth. When the Queen of the

Underworld decapitated him, he lost that ability. She decapitated him because she did not have any use for him as a statue in the Underworld.

She tossed him away; but eventually a couple of years back, she did make use of his head and him by turning him into a door knocker. Leo was always a door knocker since creation. This is one of the reasons why he has an angry attitude. He is always staring at the same components in the same place on a twenty-four hour, seven day basis.

He is often deriding the folks that walk up to him for that reason. Beside persona, character, and facial distinguishments between both Leo and Leonard, one can distinguish them in eye color, the eye lens, and their skin color. Leo has an older skin appearance. Instead of having a glimmering gold appearance, he has a bronze appearance. He has red eyes, which is indicative to his birthplace, that place being the Underworld.

His eye lenses have an odd appearance. Instead of having two corneas and pupils in each eye, he has one pupil and one cornea per eye. His pupil is darkish blue color to indigo. His cornea is light red. Leonard has a different ocular and skin appearance. His gold looks on a daily basis like it has emerged from a polishing factory. His gold glimmers so much to the point of it being invaluable and unsellable. He has light green to aquamarine colored eyes, which is indicative that he enjoys supernatural effects because the eyes are constantly blinking. He has two pupils and two corneas in each eye.

Each cornea and pupil being a different color. The upper right pupil in his right eye is red; and the color of the upper right cornea in that same eye is sapphire. The lower left pupil in his right eye is brown; and the left cornea in the same eye is green. The left eye has a yellow pupil with a teal color cornea, those colors are for the upper left pupil and cornea.

The lower right pupil and cornea have a white and black color; the white color for the pupil and the black color for the cornea. He has a variety of colors for his pupils and cornea to match his whimsical and interesting personality. Leo has a very raspy voice, one of the reasons to show his demeanor. His voice sounds very hoarse and abrupt. In a polar opposite fashion, Leonard has a voice that is vivacious, joyful-sounding and filled with sheer ecstacy. Leonard does not have a mane, in spite of being a male lion; but he does have a flip-style hair appearance on the top of his head. His flip is approximately six inches in height. Leo, however, does not have a flip. Rather, he has the appearance of an older, rancorous lion, with a mane. His mane is not well-groomed. The designer who created the statue

make his mane look unkempt and disheveled. The alien leader's wife and her cousin-in-law walked up to the double doors, and stared at the door knockers for precisely one minute. Wilheim looks wide-eyed, staring in fascination at both lions, trying to analyze them and understand them.

Rubi is showing a face of fury. Her hands are positioned in the forms of fists. Veins are showing in her forehead. And her teeth are clenching. She is grinding her teeth. The alien leader's cousin is completely oblivious to what is about to happen to him. He is just continuing to stare at both lions and he is giving a skeptical expression in the way they appear to him. Rubi's anger is increasing.

The fuel is being added to the fire. She is raising her fist. She is clenching her teeth in a stronger fashion. She raised her hand the first time. She looked right. Five hundred feet away, Light is still present on the track. She halted her punch. She is becoming even more furious. She is grunting. She raised her hand a second time. She looked at Light, still being in fear that he would eradicate her if she threw a punch at Wilheim. Enkel emerged from the Celestial City.

"Stop! Rubi, stop. You can change your ways now. Maybe, some folks won't believe you. Maybe, you might end up in jail; but Rubi, you can change, you have the opportunity right now. I know you might have some evil in your heart; but we can eradicate it and purify your heart so you're angelic like me", he said with a smile.

He strummed his musical harp.

"No, I am not listening to you. Wilheim deserves to be punched because if he's going to stare at these creepy- looking lions all day then, he's wasting my time. I have to go to the Underworld to free Jacqueline. I must see the queen, her sister. I must be able to do those things. Stop harassing me, you nuisance scrub. You are a pathetic individual, who should be ashamed of herself. You are animalistic. You are nothing but this supernatural perfectionist, who claims that he can just come down from the Celestial City. You think who you are. You are a relentless, pathetically annoying individual. So, maybe, you should go back to where you belong", replied the alien leader's wife.

He strummed his harp once again.

"Rubi, do you understand what I am saying? I am trying to help you. I am not here to hurt you. I am here to enhance your being in the afterlife. Do you want to spend eternity down here, where Jacqueline is located in the Underworld, known as Hell? Is that what you want to happen?" asked the angel.

"Quite frankly, I don't care where I go in the afterlife. All I care about is that either myself or the Blanco Brothers have the agenda done, that agenda being to kill Will and Wilheim. That's all we want to do. That agenda is our goal. We don't care if the whole crowd surrounds us and starts shootinng rays at us. We don't care if we go to the Underworld in the after life. So, you can shut your piehole if you want to do that", answered Rubi.

"So, you don't care about the after life, eh? How come such a thing is the case? Do you think you have anything to lose? Do you think that the Underworld is the greatest place to visit? Do you even want to see what's inside the Underworld? Do you think you will win with your sinister attitude? Do you want to understand what it's like in the Underworld?" asked Enkel.

"I'll answer your questions; but then, you'll have to answer my question. To answer your first question, I really don't give a crap about the after life. To answer your second question, I do think the Underworld is one of the more fascinating places to visit. To answer your third question, I do not have anything to lose and this is the case because it's simply the case, I want to see the Underworld. The only thing I want to win is to have my agenda fulfilled, that agenda being the Leader of Starmos City with Will and Wilheim dead. To answer your last question, hopefully your last question, I do want to understand and see what's inside the Underworld. Now, that I've answered your questions, I hope you are happy and shut up. The question I have to ask is what does the Underworld have to do with the one above?" asked the alien leader's wife.

"It doesn't have anything to do with the one above. It's just that bad individuals who violate good commands and cause trouble while being alive as an alien or human will wind up in the Underworld. The Underworld is where the demons live. Hell is worse than the Underworld because in Hell, one is constantly burning with the devil, who is a tad worse than a demon. Anyway, Rubi, I am talking to you to make a point. And that point is, there is a better place than the Underworld or Hell. It's called the Celestial City, the city filled with pure white and gold. It's your choice if you want to go there", answered the angel.

"Well, it's your choice to get out of here. I would personally appreciate it if you'd just scurry along and float back up to where you belong; but, if you want to stay, that's your prerogative. You have a choice. I don't think your infiltration on my personal space is acceptable", replied the alien leader's wife.

"Well, that's fine. I can accept the individuals who refuse to speak with me. Your pejorative behavior is not respectable and it certainly does not fly by with me. It doesn't impress me, with your hard-headed, agenda fulfilling, elitist attitude. Your attitude is a threat to my ideology. What you sew, you shall reap.

Your reward will not be the Celestial City. Rather, it will be the Underworld. Your reward will not be a white and gold structures being held on a billow of clouds. Rather, your reward will being place in a crystalized immobile cell. You will not be able to move in this cell because if you're so fascinated with the Underworld, you might as well make yourself a part of the Underworld. I think I shall carry on with my time here. You are on your own. See ya'. No, wait. I meant, I won't see you. The reason why is because your going to be stuck in what's that place called? Oh, I think I know the answer to that, the Underworld", he said in a strong demeanor. He smiled as he floated back up to the Celestial City. The Demon emerged from the Underworld. Jacqueline, the demon, impaled the pitchfork in Rubi's left shoulder. She showed a sinister smirk after she did this. "What did you do that for?" asked the alien leader's wife.

"Because I felt like that. Why did you argue with Enkel?" asked Jacqueline.

"Because he was bringing an argument with me. He was acting in such a pathetically absurd manner. He was acting ridiculous. He was acting in a strong-headed egotistical manner. He thought who he was. So, I had to argue my point with him! Then, he made me feel guilty, like I belong in the Underworld. He was trying to tell me that I don't belong here and was strumming this ridiculously absurd harp, although I must admit it did sound quite elegant.

He was being relentless and harassing the living guts out of me. When I told him to cut it out, he refused to listen. He just continued being a nuisance. He continued acting in such an absurd manner. He continued showing such utter disrespect towards my rights. Then, what aggravated me the most was that he was extremely sarcastic to me. He was saying what I sew, it would come back to haunt me. My agenda is to kill Will. It has always been. And it always will be. To basically be concise with you, Enkel was annoying me to the boiling point. So, I told him to skamper off. He left. Then, you came", said Rubi.

"I can totally understand where you're coming from. Now, the reason why I came down was to give you the carte blanche to assault Wilheim. Punch him and knock him out. Make sure he's unconscious to the point where he can be sent to the Crystal Cell in the Underworld. Then, I get to go free. And we get to have our agenda fulfilled. When I go free, we will be able to cause the trouble. We will be able to cause collateral damage to Will's Leadership. Hence, we will be able to gain control of Starmos City and have our justice. We will be the ones to eradicate every single one of the citizens and foreigners who've participated in the rebellion against Cornelius. Additionally, when we take over, we will be able to get the ones who helped in the revolution. Then, to go even further, we might be able to take control over the World, every universe, and every dimension. Five years after our leadership, we will be able to have total control over anything to everything. We will be able to control movement, life, death, minds, and existence. We will be able to rule for good and ever unless some psychopathic, deceitful, deceptive, malicious smart ass like Will wants to remove us from our spot. Then, we will be screwed. Wait. I've just remembered, Will is going to be dead. So, we won't have to worry about anybody who has a chip on his or her shoulder against us. We will be the ones to revel in the experience for taking over everything", replied Jacqueline.

An evil, hearty laugh left her mouth after she said this. Rubi also laughed in an evil but quiet manner.

"Thank you so much. You have done a lot more good for me than that damn Enkel. All he knows how to do is open his mouth. You know how to get things done and boost morale. You have just increased my spirits. I will punch Wilheim right now. Thank you so much", she said.

"Oh, no problem. anytime", replied the demon.

She disappeared and returned back to the Underworld. Immediately after, Rubi punched Wilheim right in the head knocking him out. She turned her head to the right. Light has shapeshifted into a robot. He is charging at the alien leader's wife with great force.

"Don't you dare go kill Will's cousin. You do not have any right to do such a thing", he yelled.

He charged at her with his fists straight in the air. She twisted his arm and flipped him over. THUD, a loud noise was heard on the floor. She flipped Wilheim once again after she flipped Light to make sure he, in particular was unconscious. BANG! The noise of the floor rattled as he was flipped. Leo started laughing.

"You did a great job knocking out those numb skull imbeciles. I felt like I was surrounded by idiots when they were in my ocular presence", he said.

"Of course, you are the one who is consistently laughing when negative things take place. Why do you always have to be the one that does that?" asked Leonard.

"Can't you give the old, ratchety fellow a break? Can't you give the brass looking, red-eyed, unkempt lion a break? No, wait, I forgot, you were my annoying neighbor. You were the one who likes to aggravate me", said the old lion. "Don't make like you're so old. You were just made with bad quality, that's all. It's really not a big deal. Don't feel embarrassed. Hey, look at my eyes", replied the vivacious lion.

"Oh, yes, look at your bizarre eyes, which belong in the circus. How do you like an insult like that? Don't tell me that I have an awful appearance simply because I am made of an older kind of gold and being that I am worn out. Stop deriding me, you World class clown", said Leo.

"Alright, I don't think there's any need for insults to be thrown back and forth to eachother, I think we need to get the point across here. We need to discuss how we are going to handle the one visitor right here, this lovely lady", replied Leonard.

"Don't say she's so lovely. Her arguing was not lovely. I found it quite pathetic that she was speaking with a ridiculously annoying angel and pathetically sinister demon. However, I must admit one thing, she is quite funny. After punching those two idiots and showing her teeth grinding fury, that behavior I like. It's neither too draconian to be disturbing nor is it too boring for one to close the eyes. It was funny. Those two probably got what they deserved, a punch in the face", said Leo.

"Now, I know that you have knowledge of what's right versus what's wrong. How can you possibly say it's okay for one to strike another simply because she's being annoyed? You know it's not funny. So, why are you laughing?"

Leonard asked in a nonchalant high-pitched voice.

"Don't you know how to be respectful to me? It's my right to laugh at whatever I want to laugh at. It's my right to be as brusque as I want to be. It's my right for me to deride whoever I want to deride. It's my right to..", the older lion was interrupted by the vivacious lion.

"And it's my right to interrupt you when you're wrong. It's my right to determine if find good things funny. It's my right to be happy. It's my right to be jovial, even though my head his mounted to this door. It's my right to simply be, Leonard."

He finished speaking. He shifted his eyes toward Leo. As he did that, he raised his eyebrows.

"Oh, you're so right", Leo said sarcastically.

"Would you mind letting me in here?" asked the alien leader's wife.

"No, I am not going to let you in here. I don't care how funny I find you to be. Besides, you are nothing but an idiot if you make me laugh", answered the old lion.

"You're calling me an idiot? What have I done to be called an idiot? I don't think that label should be slapped on my face because I can say plenty of things about you that you may not want to hear. How does that sound?" asked Rubi.

"I don't really care. I've had a lot of names be thrown at me my entire life. They say, 'sticks and stones won't break my bones; but names will never hurt me.' That applies to me", answered Leo.

"Now, I hate those that like to bring up a bunch of bullshit proverbs. There's not any need for that. I've already dealt with somebody who pulled that shenanigan and I've already taken care of that individual. Don't let me have to take care of you", replied the alien leader's wife.

"What are you going to do to me? Please tell me so I can laser you with my eye sockets and give you a third degree burn. Come on. I want to hear from your bellicose mouth", said the old lion.

"You can't do that to me. I am adroit. I have the capacity to move. You don't I can climb these walls in here. Hide behind your laser shots through the arches and even behind the arches", replied Rubi.

"You can't hide from me. You just can't.

It's absolutely, unequivocally physically impossible to do such a thing", said Leo.

"Why is that the case?" asked the alien leader's wife.

"Because those who are in hiding will eventually have to come out. You know that you can't just be a sedentary rock. A mobile alien must be constantly moving around because he or she will eventually freeze up and become in a state where one would not want to be in", answered the old lion.

"What state would that be?" asked Rubi. "A state where you're immobile. A state where you can't move one bit. A state where you'd feel uncomfortable even if you did try to move. A state that is consistently making you feel like you're in excruciating, searing, mind- numbing pain. Do you want such a thing to happen?" asked Leo.

"Absolutely not", answered the alien leader's wife.

"Then, there are two things that you can do. Either, you can show respect to me and not have to worry about being shot with the laser or you question me, show utter disrespect towards me, and dishonor me and take the shot like a man", replied the old lion.

"What would you call somebody being

disrespectful to me?" asked Rubi.

"Why would you be asking me such an absurd question?" asked the Leo. "Because I can ask that kind of a question. I don't find it absurd or ridiculous. I don't find it to be something pathetic like your condescending attitude believes it to be", answered the alien leader's wife.

"You see? Your attitude right there is showing me utter disrespect. The way you're questioning me about my attitude shows me that you are somebody who has a challenging and questioning demeanor. I don't like somebody like you. You better show me respect or else", said the old lion.

"I have a great deal of respect for you. Was I not the one who entertained you and made you laugh? Who else makes you laugh? I don't think too many folks do such a thing because I am sure you feel miserable as hell showing that puss on your face staring in a stone-faced manner. You always have an attitude that somebody is causing exasperation in you", replied Rubi.

"You can shut up now. You are acting like an ignorant idiot. Why don't you just listen to me and skamper off where ever you came from because you are just being plain relentless. You want to go behind these double doors so that way you can go see what's back there. I don't think so. As long as I'm living an outsider who visits the Underworld is not welcome because they might free somebody from the Underworld. I don't want anything to happen to Starmos City", said Leo.

"You cannot tell me what to do. If I want to come in, then I can come in. I am just here to pay a visit. I am not here to disturb the dead or cause a massive disruption. I am not here to bring in superstitious gifts, which can cause the supernatural to happen. I am not here to release anybody because I certainly do not want anything to happen to Starmos City."

She paused, then continued.

"Yeah, I don't want anything happening to Starmos City because that's simply the place where I live. Do you think for one second I want something to happen to my house? The answer is, 'no'.", said Rubi.

She lied through her teeth as she made this statement. She smirked as she made this statement. Leo didn't realize what she'd just said and the way she conducted herself in making that statement.

"Well, I don't care what you want to tell me; but I must tell you something if you let me make my statement. There are some folks who have different ideologies, beliefs, theories, ideas, or anything in their mind. These folks have these different beliefs because it's simply their belief. There are some folks who don't take chances like myself. So, let me be clear with you on this. I don't care how much you beg, plea, or do whatever to have yourself allowed access to the Underworld. With me as the guard, that is not going to be the case. I am not going to give you any access. You need to learn to just grin and bear my result. If you have a problem with me, you can learn to take it up with me. Perhaps, maybe you should listen, and then you'll learn something for yourself. Maybe, my ideologies might someday become your ideology, where we don't take chances. However, I don't think that's going to happen. I can see it's not going to happen. I can see that your hard- headed, narrow-minded, elitist attitude is going to get you far", he said.

Leonard started moving his knocker. KNOCK, KNOCK, KNOCK. The noise sounded at least quiet. Three more loud knocks were sounded. Both Rubi and Leo are still arguing.

"Cut it out, both of you! You two are being extremely immature and disrespectful. How can you two act this way with me? Your behavior is an absurdity. It goes to show that you don't know the meaning of respect. Leo, you stop preaching your rhetoric about not letting outsiders in because that attitude really needs to stop. You, Rubi, shut the hell up! All you're doing is causing a loud ruckus through your ridiculous and pathetically idiotic quarrel. You two are bickering back-and-forth about inconsequential information. I don't feel like dealing with this nonsense from you imbeciles", yelled Leonard.

"This is an A and B Conversation. So, see ya' way out of it", said the old lion. "Keep your mouth closed. I can see my way into the conversation whenever I want to. It's my prerogative. If you want to annoy me, you can very well do that. I am just going to keep my lively self. You, Leo, are not a lively individual. Rubi, you are a very argumentative and confrontational lady. All you know how to do is show belligerence and consistently argue. You are pathetic in your attitude. You should be ashamed of yourself with your idiotic demeanor. You just think who the hell you are when you enter here. I don't like that kind of pathetic attitude", replied the vivacious lion.

"Leo, keep your mouth shut. Same here for you, Leonard. You need to learn to mind your own business. You need to learn to keep your nose out of situations where you do not belong. This argument was between me and Leo. Did I ask for you to roll in? I didn't think so. I didn't ask for your loud pathetic and simpleton-like mouth to enter this conversation. Your behavior is an absurdity. The only thing you know how to do Leonard is act extremely immature. You do not have any intelligence because you are always acting in a bubbly manner", said the alien leader's wife.

"I am not bubbly. Do I look bubbly? I didn't think so. I can be a smart ass just like you. However, I chose not to. I try to keep the peace as much as possible. Unlike you, I try to avoid trouble and aggravation", replied Leonard. "Yeah, you're certainly doing a good job with regards to trying to not aggravate me. I can see where this is going. You're trying to avoid trouble and not cause ridiculousness to take place", Rubi said in a sarcastic manner.

She laughed and made a deriding remark after she acted sarcastic to him.

"So, where were we with our fight? Yes, so, I do not let any outsiders in. Come on and test my patience. It's your right if you want to do such a thing. I just want you to get the hell out of here so I don't have to see you. You are nothing but an aggravation in my life. I am sure you've heard of the burden. Yes, it's you. Wait. I forgot about my brother being a burden. He's more of a burden than you are. Rubi, you are nothing but an insignificant woman who doesn't have any meaning to be alive. So, I might consider letting you into the Underworld", said the old lion.

"I don't know what you're talking about. You are making a ridiculous statement. Whatever just came out of your mouth was stupid. It sounded so much like gibberish, it wasn't even funny. I certainly didn't find the statement you've just made to be amusing. I found it to be ridiculous and absurd. Don't ever make a statement like that with me ever again. It sounded like a two-face statement. One second you say that I am not welcome into this place. The next second, you say come on in. Well, what is it? Should I come in or not? Why did you say such a crazy one hundred eighty just now", replied the alien leader's wife.

"I know I didn't say anything ridiculous; but I did make a complete . You can enter through here. I want you to die", said Leo.

"Well, guess what? I am not going to die. I am invincible. The only way I can die is if somebody shoots me with a ray gun. If somebody does that or poisons me with excessive amounts of poison, then that's how I die. Otherwise, I can survive anything to everything. If I am decapitated, my voice box will work an I can just easily call for help to have my head reattached. If I am hung, I can swing back-and-forth and just return back to the stool. If I am buried, I can try to escape. And if I have a lack of nutrition, I can just continue walking and hunt desperately for food. I will, however, end up in a state of hunger", replied the alien leader's wife.

"Don't think you're so invincible around me. The lasers that I have can possibly kill you. To some aliens, they were lethal and they died because of that. I can tell you that not any of them have ended up in the Underworld, where you'd like to pay a visit to", said the old lion.

All of a sudden, red lasers started being fired.

"You can't get me now, old man. You don't know how to get me. Your ocular strength does not have any match for my invincibility. Come on, give me your best shot, I'll whoop you", replied the alien leader's wife.

"Alright, I will use both eyes to shoot you", said Leo.

He is shooting double lasers. Two every millisecond. The arches are being burnt. There are char marks being seen across the stone arches.

One laser almost melted through an entire stone. Then, one of the lasers touched a chandelier and bounced back, hitting him in the face.

"My eyes! My eyes! It's all your fault if I go blind. Because of you, for the rest of my life, my vision is going to be impaired. Do you want that to happen?" he asked.

"To be honest with you, I don't really care. You can die. Your behavior is uncalled for. All you know how to do is run your ridiculous and insulting mouth. You are acting immature and stupid. You do not have any meaning to be around me. All I am just doing is using you to get what I want. Do you think I give a crap about your problems?" asked Rubi.

"I don't care if you care about my problem. You are not important to me", answered the old lion.

"Both of you, cut it out. You two are acting like immature individuals. Now, Rubi, can you do me a favor?" asked the vivacious lion.

"And what favor would that be?" asked the alien leader's wife.

"Can you answer this one question for me? And I will persuade my brother into letting you have access into this place. The favor I ask is can you give me your reason as to why you want to be..?"

Leonard was interrupted by the stentorian voice of the one. The one who is featured on the massive mirror screen. The one who has the ultimate authority of granting access to folks who enter, the only Elitrionic. On the screen, he has a theatrical mask-like appearance.

The sides of his face are curved. There aren't any rigid parts about him. His face mask is the color of ghost white. His eyes are oval and rounded. Neither does he have ears or hair. He does not have any neck or body. He only has a face. He is only a face mask.

"Who is to enter the Underworld Dimension?" he asked.

"It is I, Rubi Von Alien", he answered.

"You're one of our own. I never heard of a Rubi Von Alien. I didn't know I had a Von Alien in my family", answered Elitrionic.

"Were you born into the Von Alien Family or were you married and became a Von Alien?" asked the face mask.

"I was married as a Von Alien", answered the alien leader's wife.

"Really? What was your maiden name?" asked Elitrionic.

"Rubi Worschinskiwitz", answered Rubi.

Elitrionic is researching the alien leader's wife's maiden name.

"You must me married to Will, the savage who stole my spot from the throne. Who does he think he is? I bet you my annoying pathetic cousin is trying to run the throne. I shouldn't call him my cousin. Who does he think he is to just take ove my throne? I bet you he killed Jacqueline. You were probably sent down here to destroy the Underworld, where I live. You are nothing but a beast", said the face mask.

"Excuse me? I am not here to destroy anything. I am not here to cause trouble. In fact, I am here to help the Underworld", replied Rubi.

"No, you are probably tricking me. You took your husband's side because when I invited him to move in with me in the Alien Estate, after I killed his parents. You saw what he did to me. He placed me in this position as a dead man, as Elitrionic. What did all the citizens do after I died? Celebrate? Have a jubilee?" asked the face mask.

"Oh yes, the citizens did celebrate. They celebrated the fact that you died and they wanted to show honor towards your life. They honored you for being their great leader and place Will in jail", answered the alien leader's wife.

She lied through her teeth as she made that statement. Her evil soul wants her to believe that.

"No, really? I thought my citizens hated me. I thought they would have been singing if I left life. I thought they would've been rejoicing and basking in the joy if Will killed me", replied Elitrionic.

"Well, they didn't", said Rubi.

"Now, I don't want to get into the nonsense because I can see this conversation is not going anywhere. Would you mind giving me your purpose as to why you are coming down here? It's not like you would come down here for any reason. Everybody who comes to this station arrives with a purpose. So, why don't you tell me what your purpose is?" asked the face mask.

"Okay. You would never think this. And I don't think you would even believe me on this. This is not undercover to you, the Blanco Brothers, Wilheim, and Light. This is undercover to everybody else. So I can have the ability to take over the estate and bring everything back to the way you led this city, I am going to assassinate Will, Wilheim, and Light. I am going to have those three eradicated so that way there's not any way they could come after me and charge me with any crime. I want everything to be brought back the way you led the city, in a tyrannical manner", answered Rubi.

"It is one thing to kill a dissident. It's another thing to kill your own. How could you want to kill your own? You supposedly stood by with him? Jacqueline told me you stood by with him", replied Elitrionic.

"There were only a few reasons why I stood by with him. The first reason was so that way I can receive all the luxuries a first lady can receive. The second reason was so that way I can gain power over the city. And the third way was so that way I can kill Will and his cabinet without anybody suspecting", said the alien leader's wife.

"That's a surprise. Can you tell me what exactly you're going to do in this Underworld?" asked Elitrionic.

"I am going to kill Wilheim or have him imprisoned depending on how I feel at the moment. Then, I am going to have Jacqueline set free, have you set free, and then I am going to have the Leader of the Underworld, Jacqueline's sister help me in my taking over of Starmos City and reviving the old regime", answered Rubi. "That sounds pretty reasonable to me. On behalf of the Underworld, I hereby grant you unlimited access. Welcome. Comeon in", said the face mask.

He opened the doors causing the knockers to open their mouths.

"Thank you so much", shouted the alien leader's wife.

The doors opened, and she dragged Wilheim past the doors. As she dragged him, a sinister laugh left her mouth.

Chapter IX: Fammer Alley Road

It is now five in the morning, Underworld Time. The Underworld does not seem dark and gloomy as of yet. It doesn't seem like the evil souls are out or imprisoned in the Secret Lair in the Scarlet Castle. The dimension has a blank appearance. The alien leader's wife is walking through a strong cloud of greyish black mist.

The mist feels very strong to the point where it causes water droplets to emerge from the skin pores. The water droplets are not sweat. When the mist reaches physical contact of any object, water will emerge from that particular object. There's 100% mist in this area. One is not able to see what's in here. The air in this mist feels very thick, and the dew point is high in this area.

The temperature in the mist area feels extremely cold. The plants featured around here are unkempt thorn bushes and thistle shrubs. There's an abundance of plants with wide leaves and plants that belong in the tropics exist over in this area. In spite of all this mist being in existence, there is not any rain in this dimension. The sun is always shining. The mist is also ephemeral. The mist only lasts for one hour from half past four to half past five in the morning.

The alien leader's wife is walking along a rocky path. The waterfalls are not filled with any water because there hasn't been any deceased bodies in the Underworld. There are two waterfalls at the entrance of the Underworld. The waterfalls stand at nineteen feet in height. In this area, there's a swamp leadiing to the entrance of the castle. One would think this dimension comprises of the castle. However, that's not the case.

This dimension comprises of several streets. A large number of streets are used for the Houses of the Deceased. Some are used for shops. The Underworld Dimension only has one physical occupant. Either there are ghosts, entombed individuals who've ended up in the wrong place at the wrong time in their life, or individuals who wanted to end up down here or were predestined to end up here.

Rubi is walking through the mist. The temperature is starting to increase as she becomes closer into the dimension. It is now 85 degrees fahrenheit, she is starting to sweat. All of a sudden, there's a part of the rocky walkway that is obscured by vegetation. There's a thorn tree, which is blocking this entrance. Surrounding the thorn tree are different tall native weeds and native tropical plants.

There are not any orchids down here

because the queen forbade them from being in existence since they were too peaceful for this area. The rocky trail is more serpentine as she's walking down. There are some loose rocks. Closer to the end of the trail, where the vegetation is located, she is becoming more conscientious of loose rocks.

She is constantly looking at the ground. There are more loose rocks. Eventually, she's becoming closer to the vegetation. As she is becoming closer, she is becoming more nervous. She's thinking to herself, why did she go down here in the first place? She is starting to regret entering simply because of the loose rocks. She changed her feelings and ten seconds later, dismissed the loose rocks being in existence.

She walked in a more brisk fashion. Fortunately, she did not slip as she walk. About five feet before reaching the vegetation, a boulder trips her and causes her to fall into a three foot muddy ditch. The mud feels extremely moist. Her hair is partially dirty. The cleanliness of her clothing has been soiled. She has not reacted, feeling too nervous to open her mouth. Eerie sounds are being heard.

Constant hissing from above. The vegetation above her is moving. Her nervousness and fear are inceasing. Her jaw and her entire body locked up as this took place. The vegetation is moving further. The volume of the constant hissing from above is increasing. All of a sudden a moving tail is emerging from the tree. This tail has a scaly appearance. The tail retracted. She is becoming wide-eyed. She is looking at the vegetation in shock. The tail re-emerged from the vegetation above. The tail is moving once more.

Eventually, the snake fell from the tree tops and disintegrated into the soil. The alien leader's wife bounced back, hitting the wide-birch tree behind her. The snake re-emerged from the soil. He has a ghost like appearance. He fell on the floor. When the alien leader's wife bounced against the tree, she ended up in a state of unconsciousness. About thirty seconds later, she returned back to her normal state of consciousness, she blinked her eyes. She has awakened. The snake slithered up to her face.

"What do you want? Who are you?" she asked.

"You don't remember me? How can you not remember me? I was the one who assassinated one of your husband's best friends? What are you doing here in this Underworld? What gives you the right to come down here?" asked the serpent.

"You didn't answer my question first. I want to know who you are and I want to know what your purpose is of spooking me. You are to answer my question first before I answer your question", answered Rubi.

"Fine. I just want to tell you that your attitude is so audacious. I am Serpianto. My brother Korbian is in the Crystal Cell because he was the active shooter. I was juut the mastermind. Still, I was executed as a human. My shapeshifting abilities still exist in this area. I can still turn into a serpent or a human if I want to, a ghost like one, that is. I think I answered your question very well", Serpianto replied in a smart aleck manner.

"Now, let me answer your question. I clearly remember you. I pretended not to like you just so I can stay in the estate and have some power over Starmos City. You were unknowingly fulfilling my duty and my agenda. Get rid of Will's confidants. Then, get rid of him. I am down here for two reasons. First, to get back the power of Starmos City, to fulfill Elitrionic's leadership. Second, to free Jacqueline, her sister, Elitrionic, and to kill Will and his cabinet. Those are my goals; and I will get them done without any obstruction. Now, can I ask you why you spooked me?" asked the alien leader's wife.

"I spooked you for a couple of reasons. First, to get my point across by showing oblivious folks that this is an intimidating place; and it's too late for them to leave. I didn't find that you were intimidated. I am not trying to cause you to be detained in this Underworld forever because you will be fulfilling the agenda that I want. I am the only one who can give folks the key out of this Underworld, that is if they don't meet the queen. Now, the second reason why I spooked you was because I was trying to be funny", answered the serpent.

He laughed as he made this statement.

"Well, how long will it take me to get into this city? I don't feel like sitting in here all day or having to trudge the a dense jungle all day", replied Rubi.

"Once you come out of these trees, which will be in about ten feet, you will be arriving at the grey brick road. This road has a name. Fantom Road, I remember the name. Fantom Road is the road that turns and leads up to the Scarlet Crystal Castle. Jacqueline's Sister, I believe, runs the Castle. Unfortunately, she doesn't know that her sister is imprisoned here. I've heard it that she is frozen in the Secret Lair's Crystal Cell. It's going to be extremely hard for you to free her from there. You better be very careful in front of the queen. You must show her the utmost loyalty because she hates anybody who's an alien. She wil not think twice about turning you into one of us. I'd suggest you'd show her a ton of royalty and instead of calling her by her name, you are to address her as, 'your majesty' or 'your highness.' You are to be kind to the queen even though she is very bigoted about her views on the aliens entering this dimension.

She deserves the utmost respect", said Serpianto.

"Thank you very much", replied the alien leader's wife. "No problem. I am going to conclude my time with you because I have to move on with my day. I have some other issues to handle. Just come out of those woods. Hail the horse cart and you will be driven to Scarlet Crystal Castle", said the serpent.

He returned back into the vegetation and Rubi continued down the trail. All of a sudden, she removed some of the vegetation and saw a large amount of brightness.

She walked into that brightness; and officially landed in the Underworld. She started walking into the Underworld. She is walking down a street that zig-zags. The buildings on this street stand at sixty feet. The sky in the Underworld is dark blue with grey clouds. She is walking on a cobblestone road. The zig-zag road moves upwards.

The ghosts are walking into the different stores. Above these stores, are apartments. The apartments are used to house the poor ghosts who did not have enough money to afford a house. Also, the ghosts who are awaiting sentencing to Hell are forced to stay into these apartments by the one above. There are about one hundred shops and restaurants on these streets. The restaurants are on the South Side of the street, where Rubi is located and the shops are on the North Side of the street. The street over here is adjacent to Fantom Street. This Street is called Fammer Alley Road.

Fammer Alley Road is named after Fammer, the famous ghost, who founded the Underworld's commercial district. To be considered an alley in this land the buildings have to be condensed, and there has to be a narrow pathway within the alley. The narrow pathway is seven feet wide. There are approximately one thousand ghosts in this area. One can clearly see the ghosts.

They do not float. Most of the ghosts are shopping and dining over here, having breakfast. Then, there are some who are heading to work. About 25% of the ghosts, in the Underworld work. All of the ones that do work, have jobs in this Alley. 75% of the ghosts were affluent and quite often shopped. Their affluence carried with them, in their immortal states.

The alien leader's wife is walking in the alley. There are differently themed restaurants. On the right side, is W. Ridley's Coffee Shop. W. Ridley's Coffee Shop is owned by a ghost, who lived in the 1700s but died in the American Revolution in 1775 because he was a traitor. He ended up in the Underworld. He was affluent and when Fammer was building this alley, W. Ridley (Walter Ridley) opened a coffee shop up here being that coffee was his specialty, in his mortal life. W. Ridley's Coffee Shop has a dark green awning with white letters in a generic font. The sign's letters are capitalized.

Often, the citizens of the Underworld pay a visit to his shop to purchase a coffee, sometimes two, or to spend quality time with each other. Adjacent to W. Ridley's Coffee Shop, is Aberman's Bake Shop. Aberman's Bake Shop hosts the generic baked goods and the special ones that come from different regions in the World. These baked goods are sold fresh on a daily basis. Aberman came from New York and moved to the Underworld, which caused him to turn into a ghost over time.

Then, adjacent to this restaurant/ shop is Brown's Breakfast Bar. Brown's Breakfast Bar is named after a healthy individual who ate an unbalanced diet and caused himself to wind up in this dimension. He opened his own business to promote healthy food such as granola bars. January is his peak month because some folks who live here are trying to come back from the dead.

These three places of business are located in an alcove within the alley, that alcove being considered a sub alley. All their doors touch eachother. In front of the bake shop, there aren't any windows other than on the door. The alien leader's wife is dragging Wilheim in the street. The ghosts are giving her an odd appearance. They are wondering what she's bringing with her. Some are disregarding her dragging of an unconscious body.

Some are choosing to look away because she is an alien and a lot of the ghosts who live here, in spite of a minority of the population being once aliens, do not have any respect for aliens and are bigoted towards the aliens of Starmos City. Across from the three quick service restaurants/ shops are three Italian Restaurants. The three Italian restaurants are differently themed for different moods and palettes.

There's a Pizzeria, which has the retrospective appearance of black and white tiles on the walls. There's a typical pizza counter with the gold and emerald tiles. In front of this counter, there's a big glass that one can see the latest styles of pizza. The latest styles displayed behind the glass on the countertop are Gorgonzola Pizza, Margherita Pie, and the Sicilian Square Pie. On the front window of the restaurant, there are gold ribbon stickers lining the sides of the window.

The restaurant is a brick building with an opening in the rooftop to remove the smoke. The restaurant has a sign PIZZERIA above the windows. This sign is made of brass. On the right of this restaurant is a more formal Italian Restaurant. Toscana is the name of this restaurant. It is a Tuscan-style restaurant. The walls of this restaurant are made of plaster. There are two alcoves that hold plants. There are fifteen tables within this restaurant and the floors are made of mosaic tile.

On the left of the pizza restaurant, there's Trattorian, more informal kind of Italian restaurant. This informal restaurant has regular table seating. However, the food is from the Southern regions of Italy. This restaurant has different pottery featured on the walls. Additionally, this restaurant has a live cooking performance. Trattorian is the name of this restaurant and the name of the region, for which the delicacies come from.

Heading further up the street, there are three Northern European Restaurants. There's a Norwegian Restaurant, which has a fireplace inside. The Danish Restaurant has arched walls and windows. The Icelandic Restaurant has more rugged walls, which represent the rugged terrain of Iceland. There are wooden floors in all three of these restaurants.

Between the Danish and Norwegian restaurants, there's a large fireplace. Hence, in the Norwegian Restaurant, there's double sources of heat, which makes this restaurant the best place to visit in the Winter months. Across the alley, from these three restaurants, there are the Central European Restaurants. The German Restaurant features a live Umpa Band and there are black, gold, and red curtains on the windows in front of the restaurant.

There's a formal bar in the center of the restaurant. Adjacent to this restaurant, is the Belgian Restaurant, which serves as a breakfast place. The left-most restaurant is the Polish Restaurant, which serves a wide variety of delicacies from Eastern Europe and Western Europe. For the different restaurants, there are different owners and different founders. The Italian Restaurants are owned by Guiliano Umbriano, who died during the revolution against the Kingdom of Italy. He was related to Umbria, the King of Italy at the time.

He was the chef at one time for the King of Italy. The one who owns the Scandanavian Restaurants is Brachekin Fjord. Brachekin Fjord was born in Iceland immigrated to Norway, and then sailed over to Denmark, later to be killed in the Great War. He was a traitor and was sent to the Underworld, where he's been living ever since. Bonn Voyagen runs the Central European Restaurants. Voyagen was born in Germany. Then, moved to Belgium and Poland.

He owned a restaurant in Germany. However, he wanted to own more and corrupted his way there. He was shot and ended up in the Underworld. There are some American Restaurants. Retroville, which is a '50s themed restaurant has a facade that is made of blue spraypainted metal. There's a Jukebox in this restaurant and there are different seating booths, which are used as tables featured inside this restaurant. The restaurant next door is an

Alaskan themed restaurant. The Orca Grill, has different fish and seafood featured on the menu.

The reason why this restaurant was named the Orca Grill was because the owner was a hunter until he became hunted. He was a nameless Eskimo. The citizens of the Underworld does not know the owner by his name. They know him because he is one of the very few introverts in town. This restaurant is made of old brick. Across from this restaurant, is Goulder's Steakhouse. Goulder's Steakhouse's building looks similar to a hunting lodge. This Building was once owned by the Goulder Family.

However, the family was struck by lightning and died after they fired their own best chef simply because he didn't want to buy the business from them. This restaurant serves 30 oz. steaks. Adjacent to this restaurant is the Bakerville Restaurant. Bakerville Restaurant is a New England style restaurant, which serves Maine Lobster and specialty clam chowders. This restaurant is located across the street from Retroville. This restaurant was owned by the Bakervin family.

The son died because he ingested a poisonous lobster, who he killed. North of the American restaurants are the Asian restaurants. There are about five Asian restaurants from different regions of Asia. The Japanese and Indian restaurants are located adjacent to one another. And the Chinese and Korean Restuarants are located across from the Japanese and Indian. Above the Asian restaurants is the Dojo, which is a massive restaurant that has a fusion themed cuisine.

The Dojo is divided into two buildings. The North Part serves North Asian Pacific Cuisine. The South Part serves Southeast Asian cuisine. As the road continues to zig-zag, the incline increases. After the restaurants, there are ten shops. There are two boutiques: one for men and another for women. There's a woman's shop for make-up and facial wear. There's a man's shop for different clothing accompaniments. It is like a haberdashery.

There's a man's shop exclusively for jewelry and a woman's shop for jewelry as well. The name of the Jewelry Stores is Scarlet Jewelers, named after the Scarlet Crystal Castle. The color of the buildings are indigo because the one who owns the buildings has an eccentric personality. The owner has very eclectic tastes with regards to design. Heading upwards, there are two blue buildings.

One building is light blue. There's an ice cream shop in the building. The name of the ice cream shop is Coneville. Coneville has been around in the Underworld for one-half of a century. There's a red and white swirl light as the logo for the restaurant. There's Golden Candy Co. across the street from the ice cream shop. This restaurant features a Candy Cane Swirl Machine, which is exclusive to this shop. This is the only store in all dimensions that has a shop like this. The Golden Candy Co. also has a Pop Swirl Machine, which there are only four across all the dimensions. Adjacent to this store is the Ghostly Strong Bank. The Ghostly Strong Bank holds all the money for the ghost population in this town.

The Ghostly Strong Bank does not print money because everything is valued in gold. Gold is really inexpensive in this dimension. This bank is made of marble stone. There's a slanted rooftop on the top of this bank. Adjacent to this bank, is the Welcome Center. The Welcome Center is a Brownstone building with a glass facade on the front. The Welcome Center has wooden floors and a polished wooden front desk. There's always an employee present at this front desk on a twenty four hour basis.

There's also an on-site host, who can give the newcomer a tour of the dimension. This place also serves a purpose for ticket purchasing for the dunebuggy to the Scarlet Crystal Castle. The street turns and leads on to Fantom Road. Fantom Road is the street to the castle. This street is not only the commercial hub and the hubbub for ghosts. This place is also the highest point in the Underworld. This alley has a land elevation of one thousand five hundred feet above ground level.

There's a long road heading to the castle from this alley. For a first time visitor, it would take about one-half hour to adapt to the environment around him or her. At the top of this street, there's a tiered fountain that is on year round because the stone will crack if it is not on for one day.

The fountain is running twenty four hours. The fountain functions similar to the way the Roman Fountains functioned because the water is moved by gravitational force. There are not any pipes moving the water. Some of the street shops are contemporary. Yet, there's a historical aura in the area. Most of the restaurants are retrospective in appearance. At the same time, most of the restaurants look new because the ghosts properly maintain them.

The alien leader's wife is walking up the street. She is looking at the shops in an odd and perplexed manner. She is walking through the ghosts. The ghosts were giving her a nasty attitude. The older male ghosts were dressed in suits. Some had plump appearances and others had rotund appearances. Then, there were those who had gaunt appearances and some who had the mundane appearances.

There aren't any destitute ghosts living in this dimension. Most of the ghosts who live here are affluent. Some are dressed in tuxedos that have handkerchiefs. While are dressed with the mundane suits and ties. Some are wearing suit jackets. Others are wearing commonplace clothing like sweaters and jeans. The female ghosts wore dresses that were either modernistic or colonial. The colonial dresses were wide with ribbons.

The modernistic dresses are more narrow. The colonial dresses made some women have a rather plump appearance. One of the ghosts is sitting on the bench in front of the W. Ridley's Coffee Shop. This individual is dressed in a brown suitjacket, courderoy pants, and a white buttoned- down shirt. He has brown combed hair and hazel eyes. He is wearing a black hat and brown boots. One cannot see the colors of his clothing because he is a ghost. This is the same for every ghost in this dimension. He is smoking a cigar and drinking coffee. He has a raspy voice when he speaks.

When he drinks the coffee, it disintegrates in his soul. The alien leader's wife sat next to him on the park bench. He is one of the very few introverted ghosts in the dimension. Rubi sat down next to him.

"Hi, sir. What's your name?" she asked.

"W. Ridley jr. Who are you? What are you doing here? Don't you belong in Starmos City?" asked the ghost.

"You didn't answer my question. I asked about your name. Can you please give it to me?" asked the alien leader's wife.

"William Ridley Jr. Just call me William. Can you please answer my question?" asked William.

"Yes, I do belong in Starmos City but I am trying to find the majesty." She paused.

"That's the reason why I am here", she answered. William lifted his coffee and sipped it for one minute. He gulped.

"You paused. If I may ask, how come?" he asked.

"Because I was trying to collect myself. I wasn't thinking straight. I've just came out of the woods to come to this dimension and it was very treacherous back there", answered Rubi.

"I can totally understand where you're coming from. I know how treacherous it is to be in the woods, especially the ones in North America. That wilderness is nasty", replied the introverted ghost.

"I've never been back there; but can you explain to me why the North American Wilderness is nasty?" asked the alien leader's wife.

"Because it's just plain nasty. The animals, the terrain, and the vegetation pose an imminent threat. Those damn scientists say it's biodiversity; but it's not. Rather, it's a nuisance that should be burnt to the ground. Half of those animals do not have any significance on that Earth. All they are there to do is kill, eat, and digest. That's all they do", answered William.

"How come you are thinking in such a way?" asked Rubi.

"Because I was killed by one of those damn beasts. That's the reason why I've ended up here in the first place", the introverted ghost answered with a feeling of negativity.

"Please, if you don't mind, can you tell me what happened? Can you tell me about the situation in it's entirety?" asked Rubi.

"Sure, my father on Earth owned the coffee shop in Manhattan. I was scouting through the state to open another shop. Coffee was very rare back then in New York. So, I wanted to go find a city that was up and coming. I went to Buffalo. All Buffalo had was the Erie Canal. As I was heading up there, I was going through a volatile wilderness. Right near Buffalo, I was heading on a trail with my horse. As I was heading on the trail, this bear belligerently approached me, knocked me off my horse. I was unarmed, no knife, no gun, not anything. This bear knocked me off my horse, scratched me with his paws. He started attacking me. He jumped on top of me and started trying to bite me and rip my face off. I was fighting him. He kept fighting harder. I was becoming more tired. He tore my throat and disemboweled my heart. I immediately died. He then swallowed me. I woke up in the Underworld, which spoke volumes of my behavior on Earth. I don't know if my father is still around, I highly doubt it. I don't even think his business is still around on Earth because none of the descendants other than myself wanted to run the business. It's still here today. So, I am continuing my father's legacy, that is in the ghost world, the Underworld. Life is hard in the Underworld because you are seeing the same clients on a daily basis; but they say, 'something is better than nothing'.", answered the introverted ghost.

"Don't complain about yourself and your business because you're lucky it's still around. There aren't any businesses in Starmos City. I want to keep it that way. Nobody over there knows it because they're too stupid to understand. The citizens of Starmos City think I am the President's best wife and my husband thinks the same about me. Wait, he is in for a rude awakening. He is not going to know what's going to hit him. He's going to be

screwed for life. He deserves to die", said Rubi.

"What kind of woman are you? Are you some sort of communist or socialist? You should be banished from here because this is the land of business. The queen lets us do whatever we want whenever we want. The only time when we have to close our businesses is if she is leaving this dimension. Then, we let her come down the alley on the chariot. She deserves to be treated like royalty because after all, she's the queen and she deserves a ton of respect. She already banished the evil ones. I am sure she would encourage this alley to be successful", replied William.

"Yeah, no, you're wrong. The queen is actually related to one of my secret confidants, Jacqueline Langyaw. Everybody in Starmos City derides her even post- mortem. She is the talk of the city. Everybody was glorifying her death. In my outer soul, I was glorifying her death and adoring my husband for killing her. However, internally, I thought my husband was nothing but a murder. I believed my husband was doing the wrong thing because she would bring Starmos City to the time when Cornelius ran it, a tyranny", said the alien leader's wife.

She smiled as she said her last sentence.

"God, help you. Now, I want to know who that dead guy is right next to you. What's his name? What's his purpose of coming here?" asked the introverted ghost.

"His name is Wilheim Von Alien. He is Will's distant cousin. He was in the coalition with Will, my husband. He tried to eradicate Cornelius; but he didn't have any guts to do such a thing because he was advised not to by the family. I believe that he was right in listening to the family. The Elitrionic told me to have him killed. Besides, he deserves to die. I decided to show some form of mercy because I am not an insensitive individual", answered Rubi.

"Oh, yes, you seem quite insensitive to me. You seem evil and malicious. You seem like a sinister individual. You belong in place more like Hell. You are quite evil", William said under his breath.

"What did you say?" asked the alien leader's wife.

She raised an eyebrow as she asked the question.

"I did not say anything and don't get unusually close to me, you rogue. Stay back. Learn some personal space", the introverted ghost answered in an angry manner.

"Fine. I need to speak with you", said Rubi.

"Oh, by the way, I've forgotten to ask you what your purpose of being here is? Can you please tell me?" asked William.

"I have a few reasons why I am here.

First, I am here to dump Wilheim and have him killed. Second, I am here to free Jacqueline and Elitrionic from their prisons. Thirdly, I am here to rescue Jacqueline's sister. Fourthly, I am here to round up an army to kill Will. I already have the Blanco Brothers doing that for me; but I need a bigger group to help me. Those are the reasons why I am here. I am here to speak with you for the purpose of directions. Where would you know where I can get to a nearest coach to take me to this castle?" asked the alien leader's wife.

"Do you have any money with you?" asked the introverted ghost.

"No, because I left it in Starmos. Wait. I think I have thirty Bucks in my pocket. I can perhaps turn that currency into your currency", answered the alien leader's wife.

"Yes, that sounds like a great idea. Now, I need to ask you a question. Do you have enough money to exchange a gold coin in here? You see, we don't have a reserve system where we just take money and tax folks on getting that money. We are not like most of the dimensions. We have our own unique form currency. You'll probably be able to head to the castle and bribe the guards to let you speak with the queen. How about we cut a deal. You turn your money into gold coins. In exchange for taking me to the castle to meet the queen and have dinner with her, you can get a free coffee and lunch at my place. That's what I will do for you if you let me go to the queen. I will wait right here for you to get two tickets and the coins", replied William.

"That sounds like a good idea. Watch Wilheim and make sure he doesn't go away because he's not dead right now. He is knocked out", said Rubi.

She started walking up the block.

"You might need something right now", shouted the introverted ghost.

"What would that be? What exactly would you want me to not forget?" asked the alien leader's wife.

"I do not want you to forget the directions to go there", answered William. She walked back down to him. "Now, just walk up the block and when you see a building with an all glass facade on the first level, that's when you'll know you've reached the Welcome Center", he said.

"Very well, then. I'll text you when I get there", replied Rubi.

"What does it mean to text somebody?" asked the introverted ghost.

"It means to send words using your Gphone", answered the alien leader's wife.

"What is a Gphone?" asked William.

"A Gphone is a communication device that you can use the internet, call friends, call family, Face eachother, send messages, and do different things", answered Rubi.

"What does it mean to make a call?" asked the introverted ghost. "It means to communicate with somebody from a long or short distance audibly, not face-to-face", answered the alien leader's wife. "I've never heard of such a thing. Can you explain that to me, further?" asked William.

"It's too complicated to explain. I will see you in five or ten minutes. Just let me carry on", answered Rubi.

She walked up the alley, dodging all the congestion. She walked up to the Welcome Center. There are four ghosts present. The Welcome Center is empty with patrons. There are two female ghosts and two male ghosts.

There's a relatively young male ghost, who is wearing knickers and a buttoned-down shirt. Standing adjacent to him is an older male ghost. He has unkempt hair in the back. He is wearing a suit jacket and a white buttoned-down shirt. One cannot see the colors of the ghosts, what they wear, their skin color, and their colors. There are two female ghosts standing next to the two male ghosts.

The older female ghost is wearing glasses, a kerchief over her head, and is knitting at her desk. The younger female ghost is wearing a dress and is wearing jewelry rings on her hands. Rubi walked up to the younger male ghost. He has a charismatic voice.

"Welcome to the Underworld dimension. How may I help you? What do you need me to do?" he asked.

"Thank you for being so nice. You are very kind for a ghost. I need you to convert these Starmos Bucks into coins. I also need to buy tickets for the Stagecoach", answered Rubi. She gave him the money.

"Sure, I'd be glad to do such a thing", replied the clerk.

He placed the Starmos Bucks into a conversion calculator. The results of the calculator stated two gold coins, each worth one hundred in the value of the Underworld. He gave her three silver coins, each worth fifty in the Underworld. She took the Silver Coins and returned back to the introverted ghost, William. "So, what did you get?" he asked. "I got three silver coins, each worth fifty, and two stagecoach tickets", answered the alien leader's wife.

"What time will the stagecoach be at the station?" asked the introverted man.

"It'll be there in about fifteen minutes", answered Rubi.

"Perfect timing. That means we can go out and have some drinks, nonalcoholic ones. I have different flavored coffees at my shop. Would you care for any specific type?" asked William.

"Sure. First, I want to see the menu. Then, I will decide on what I order", answered Rubi.

"Well, as long as you're taking me to the queen, that sounds great. I would be happy if you to do such a thing as long I see the majesty", answered the introverted man.

He and the alien leader's wife walked into the coffee shop. The place has antiquated items. Some of the items in the shop aren't used in the present time. There's a brass coffee maker. This coffee maker grinds Cacao and turns it into Coffee beans. From there, it grinds the coffee beans and turns them into coffee.

This is featured behind the counter. There's a glass wall, which shows cooking demonstrations of specialty cakes on display at the shop. The specialty cakes are not being made right now. The specialty cakes are actually in the ice box, below. There are three rows of shelves in the ice box.

The first row of shelf shows the different cheesecakes. The different cheesecakes are strawberry, cranberry, and blueberry cheesecakes. Below this particular shelf, is the filling cakes. There's the multilayered cake. The multilayered cake is six inches in height.

This cake features banana, vanilla, custard, cannoli, mint, and strawberry fillings. There's coconut crust on the top of the cake and sponge dough on the bottom of the cake. Adjacent to this particular cake is the sphere cake. This cake is an ice cream cake, which has the similar flavor of Tartufo. On the far right, is the Mississippi Mud Pie. Below this level, there are cakes, which are native to different countries.

The French Creme Brulee Cake, the German Chocolate and Caramel Cake, and the Italian Wedding Cake are the three featured items of the week. The cakes are stored behind a curved glass. There's a bar in the coffee shop. The bar has about fifteen wooden stools and literally has wooden bars, which slide down from the ceiling. The ceiling has some lights, which function on a daily basis. Once, every month, the power turns off because the lights are obsolete. The inspector never ordered the W. Ridley Jr. to order more contemporary lights. He walked behind the counter.

He gave the carte blanche for Rubi to cut the line. He served her with a delectable

Asian Spice Coffee and Mississippi Mud Pie. This shows Rubi's eclectic tastes. She is sitting in front of the window. Wilheim is laying on the bench outside. He is about to wake up. Rubi's eyes widened.

"Where am I?" he asked himself.

"Oh crap, I am in the wrong place. I must return back to Starmos City", he said in a soliloquy.

"Oh no, this ain’t going to happen. He's not going to leave me. I am going to kill the S.O.B", she said.

She retrieved a frying pan and ran outside the shop.

"Rubi! She's going to run after me", the alien leader's cousin said in nervousness.

He ran down the street.

"Ghosts, my cousin-in-law is about to attack me. He made a threatening gesture towards me. Run after him", the alien leader's wife lied through her teeth.

The ghosts laughed at her. One of them said.

"Do you think it's fools we'd be? We are no fools. You're the fool."

Everybody laughed at her. Her face became red in infuriation.

"Enough! All of you. I am here to help her. Please. I will leave the place to the third to handle", said William. W. Ridley III, W. Ridley jr.'s son has taken charge of the restaurant.

The alien leader's wife took her coffee outside the shop and discarded the cake in the garbage bin. She and William walked out of the place of business. They walked up the Fammer Alley Road. They walked to Fantom Road. The stagecoach stop at Fantom Road has a gothic appearance. There are gothic style crosses at the stagecoach stop. The bench is covered by a reddish-brown rooftop canopy.

The canopy is supported by green shale stone. There are grey stone tiles at the station. The stagecoach arrived. The stagecoach is a black stagecoach with tinted windows. The driver's seat is unoccupied. The door of the stagecoach opened. The stagecoach is horseless. Yet, the noises of horses galloping is heard.

"This is something in the supernatural", said the alien leader's wife.

"I know. This dimension is the land of anomalous occurrences. There's not your ordinary or average thing taking place here. The average taking place here is usually abnormal or sometimes grotesque. That's your average. I have never seen any normal day here for all the years I've been dead here", he laughed as he made this statement.

The invisible stagecoach driver said, "Come on in."

He has a vivacious, elderly male voice. He has a Southern accent. The alien leader's wife and her confidant entered the stagecoach.

"Where are you off to?" asked the driver.

"Scarlet Crystal Castle", answered Rubi.

The stagecoach departed to the castle.

Chapter X: Foiled, It Shall Be

The alien leader's wife and William are on board the stagecoach. The invisible driver appeared. He is wearing a black top hat along with a long, greyish-black suit jacket. He does not have any hair. Therefore, one can see his highly transparent, white scalp. He is partially rotund and plump. He opened the window from behind.

"So, who are you two?" he asked.

Rubi looked at the introverted ghost, "Should we talk to him?" she asked.

"Of course, we should absolutely do such a thing. He was friendly with us. Why not be friendly with him?" asked William.

"Because I found him to be creepy. At first, he was invisible. Then, he became visible. Now, he's just plain creepy and scary. There was sheer silence in the ride for the past fifteen minutes. We're practically halfway through the ride. We are driving to the castle in sheer silence. Let's keep it like that. Let's try and keep our mission as covert as possible. We cannot let him know the reasons why we're heading to the castle", answered the alien leader's wife.

"I don't know. My good conscious is telling me to tell him the truth. I have a good idea. Maybe, you should think outside of the box for once. Maybe, you should threaten him and intimidate him. Force him not to tell anybody about our mission. Make lethal threats to him and he won't tell anybody. Shove the threat in his face. Don't threaten him if you suspect he is either going to forget what we said or if he truly believes he is not going to tell anybody", replied the introverted ghost.

"You know what. You're right. I will do such a thing. Besides, making conversation defers somebody from thinking about the reasons why we are heading to Scarlet Castle. I am sure we have time for a five-minute diversion. I am sure we have time to see some of the residences around here, not go in them but drive past them or something like that. See them in the distance. I am sure we can do something like that", said Rubi.

She laughed when she made this statement. She is pretending to be nervous so she can hide the covert mission from the driver. The driver turned around.

"You didn't answer my question. What is your name?" he asked.

"Me or him? Who are you talking to?" asked Rubi.

"Both of you. I want to know each one of your names. Please tell me some information about you two", he said.

"Sure. I am Rubi. I come from Starmos City. I am coming to pay Verminia, the queen, a visit. I just found her name through reading a small informational guide you had stored in your vehicle. The gentleman sitting next to me, his name is William. He owns the W. Ridlley's Coffee Shop. He comes from Earth; but has been living in the Underworld for one hundred years. Him and I got to know each other today", replied Rubi.

"Yes, that's very interesting. Can you tell me what your purpose of coming here is?" asked the driver.

"My purpose of being here is that I am here to visit Verminia. The purpose for visiting her is because I want to become the Leader of Starmos City. And I am seeking her advice. William is just coming along with me on the journey. He is coming along to meet the queen because he's never met her. He feels somewhat excited about meeting her", answered the alien leader's wife.

"Do you want to know my name?" asked the driver.

"Sure. Please, feel free to tell me", said Rubi.

"My name is Iron Steel. In my past lifetime, I was an earthling. However, I moved to Garden City, shapeshifted into a swamp monster and was awaiting execution. My alias name was Monstre. I kidnapped my own friend and tried to murder him for revenge of fencing on me. The day after Gairdon died, I was accused of killing him. I was executed and was reincarnated from a muscular individual to a rotund individual. I have changed tremendously. I know I feel much happier down here than I did up there on Earth or in Garden City. That's my background", answered Iron.

"Quite an ironic name for a man who sure as hell does not look like an Iron Steel. You seem very respectable. Although I was helping Will in his mission to fight against tyranny, I only helped him because I wanted to live in the Alien Estate and take over the leadership of Starmos City. I was the one who wanted to take over the city by soft force. I am going to gain power either while I am alive or when I am dead. I will make sure somebody brings back Cornelius's agenda", replied the alien leader's wife.

"That sounds good for you. Say, do you want a tour of this area? I am sure you would enjoy it. The buildings around here are very classy and opulent. A lot of affluent folks live around here. So, are you two in?" asked the driver.

"Sure, I am sure we can take a little bit of some circuitous route. Right, William?" asked Rubi.

"Oh, yes, sure. We can do that. We certainly do have time to do such a thing", answered the introverted ghost.

He answered this question in a sarcastic manner. They are heading down to Demoner Court. The driver described the street. All the houses on the street have a gothic appearance. Each house has a dead body present. J. Rosenthal's house is four level house.

The exterior of the house has a Victorian-style appearance. The pentagon of the house features a bedroom and a kitchen alcove. There are rocking chairs on his porch and cans of beer. These cans of beer are littered all over the porch. The porch is made of green wooden floorboards. The house is a red house with picket wood on the rooftop. There's a white picket fence around the property. The grass is overgrown and there's a defunct fountain in front of the property. The fountain has been derelict for years and if one was to kick the fountain, it would fall literally into one million pieces.

There are two stairs leading up to the porch of the house. The two steps have been in a state of decadence. On the bottom step, there's a one foot in diameter, irregularly shaped hole. The windows are the older glass windows, which were utilized in the colonial-style homes. These windows are vulnerable to being shattered, not entirely on a day with extremely fluctuating temperatures.

The stone pathway leading up to the house is gradually falling apart. The interior of the house looks totally different from the exterior of the house. The interior of the house has an elegant chandelier that is obsolete. The lights are oil lamps. The living room features an elegantly carved wooden and straw couch with pillows and cushions, which have ornate design patterns on them. Behind the living room, is a generic kitchen, which looks like it was used in the mid-1800s. There's a dining room on the side of the house. The dining room has red wallpaper with gold royal leaf emblems.

The dining room has a chippendale wood table that is polished. There's a beer stain on the table. Upstairs, there are two bedrooms. The first bedroom, the grand bedroom, has a canopy bed with green drapes. The wooden dresser has beer bottles located all over. The beer bottles are empty. There's a bathroom within the house that has functional plumbing. Adjacent to this bedroom, is the guest room, which looks like it has been untouched. This bedroom has a comfortable full-sized bed. The door leading to this room always remains closed to represent its purity and constant cleanliness. The room has a dresser with a mirror, a jewelry box, and a comfortable armchair. There's also a closet within this bedroom. The bed here has a white comforter along with white sheets. There are two pillows, which have the ability to remain cold at night because of their compactness and density of the fluff. The pillows do no have feathers stuffed in them.

Rather, they have cotton. The drunk is downstairs. He is wearing the same clothing he'd worn when he died. He is drinking beer. His ghost form causes him to stand up at seven feet in height. His volatile attitude still remains. There's a plaque in front of every house describing the ghost's past life. The plaque shows the words, "J. Rosenthal. Died 1856 in South Salt Lake, Utah Territory. He died being shot by a gun. Drunks be gone." The plaque shows those words. All of a sudden, a beer bottle flew out of the house.

"Who goes here? What are you individuals doing outside? Spying on me?" he asked in anger.

"Let's start moving", Iron said in nervousness.

He started moving the stagecoach to the next house. This house has a gothic style appearance. The house looks like steps heading to the rear. There are two decks to the house.

The first deck is where the living areas are located. The second deck is where the bedroom is located. This house has crimson wooden siding.

The porch is made of old, worn-out brick. And the porch is not protected by a canopy. The porch is eight feet long by three feet in width. The porch has a rocking chair as well. The porch has bars at the bottom because that's where the arsenal is hidden. There's an arsenal of pistols, handguns, and rifles down below.

The lawn is surprisingly well-kept. The pavers are made of reddish-brown brick. There's a birdbath on the center of the lawn that is currently empty. There's a mailbox at the front of the property. The door is a white dutch style door. The windows on the door are not tinted. There's an arched window on the upper part of the door. The front of the house has two windows.

Each window has four window panes. Neither do the sides nor the back of the house have any windows. The upper level has one window, that window being for the bedroom. In the interior of the house, the kitchen is located on the side. The kitchen has a 1900s style appearance. This kitchen has wooden cabinetry, an icebox, and a wooden countertop. There's a bloody hatchet in the kitchen. The hatchet is hidden within the cabinetry. The hatchet was used by the resident, when he was living on Earth because he was a mass-murderer.

In the kitchen, there's an interesting cutting board, which has an appearance of a wooden triangle. The sides of the cutting board are rigid. The kitchen has a sink where one can easily turn a knob to use the faucet. The dining room is located adjacent to the kitchen. The dining room has yellowish-brown plaster, which has a china closet built into the wall.

The china closet has garage-style wooden doors. The china closet is currently open. There are dishes, which have the paintings of royal emblems. There are also teacups featured in this closet. The teacups are artistically designed. There are ten drinking glasses in the china closet. Five of those drinking glasses are used on a daily basis. The living room has ornately designed seating. There's a fireplace located inside the living room. The hearth of the fireplace has snake designs carved on the outside.

The hearth has white, candles in holders made of silver. The silver holders are designed with different amorphous patterns. The floor in front of the fireplace, which holds the logs, is made of tumbled brick. The bricks have a serpentine texture. The fireplace is guarded by a black mesh. The fire is currently being used.

There's a bucket of water on the side of

the fireplace and a billow hanging on the plaster wall. All the floors in this house are wooden floors. There's a carpet in the center of the room that is painted black and has a design of the royal emblem in the center. There's a coffee table in the center of the room. There are two wooden couches with cushions sewed in the wood. In the corner of the room is a Harpsichord.

The Harpsichord is playing elegant music. There's a restroom on the first floor of the house. Walking up to the second level of the house, are elegant steps. There are eight elegant, polished wooden steps, which leads the individual up to the bedroom. There are two doors leading to the bedroom. The bedroom has a wooden divider. The parents' room has a canopy bed with velvet colored drapes. The bedroom has an elegant dresser. The dresser has leaf-shaped carvings featured within. The floor has a red carpet with a gold stitched emblem.

There's a closet within this bedroom. Adjacent to this part of the bedroom, is the son's bedroom. His bedroom has a twin bed. The same exact dresser is also featured in his bedroom. There's not any closet in his room. His side and the parents side share windows. The plaque in front of the house describes the family. "The Second Generation of the Rosenthals. James Rosenthal belonged to a gang out West. He committed several train robberies. He stole over one million dollars. In a crossfire, he and his family died in the year 1908.

He carried the money with him and hired a Harpsichord pianist, who would perform on a twenty-four hour basis. All of a sudden, gunshots were heard. However, bullets did not fly out of the gun. The arsenal is actually a false arsenal. The gunshot was fake. The noise was real. It wasn't made out of a noise machine. The stagecoach continued.

"So, do you want to see any more houses?" asked Iron.

"No, thank you. Please, don't let us look at any houses. I do not want to get shot by some psycho or have bullets flying towards me. I want to be able to live comfortably. I do not want to worry about being shot. That's the last thing I want to take place. In fact, I do not even want such a thing to take place against me or William. I wouldn't mind if it happened to Wilheim or Will; but not William or I. I want to live", answered Rubi.

"Whatever. I want to basically state that the houses are gothic style homes or Victorian homes. That's just the mundane here. We are heading pretty close to the Scarlet Castle. If you're wondering why there aren't any guards standing in front of the castle, it's because the ones who were entering the Underworld were encountered by guards and the Elitrionic. The Elitrionic tries to keep the Underworld secure as possible. If you want to meet the Elitrionic, you can go downstairs and have him awakened from the dead. If you want to meet Jacqueline, who is also in the Secret Lair, she is frozen adjacent to the Elitrionic. There are some criminals held down here because Starmos City uses this place as the burial grounds for the evil ones. That's wrong that they do this because they shouldn't execute any dangerous anarchists and they shouldn't be sending them down here", said the driver.

"Good for you. I want you to go and see the queen", replied the alien leader's wife.

"Oh, no. I can't intrude on her space", said Iron.

The Scarlet Crystal Castle is translucent. Although the castle is crystal, one cannot see inside. The scarlet color of the castle was demanded at the request of Verminia. The color represents her diabolical, sinister behavior. The castle does not have a moat surrounding it.

There's an ice fountain in front of the castle. The castles towers stand out like the flowers of a peafowl. The towers are the only transparent parts of the castle. There are thirty towers, which represent the years of existance of the Underworld Dimension. The towers are shaped in the forms of obelisks so that way not anybody would be able to enter the castle through the rooftop.

The other reason why the towers are shaped in the form of obelisks is because of a superstition that obelisks are able to absorb lighting and produce electricity. That particular superstition has not been verified. Additionally, the towers are symbolic in that they represent the majesty and power of the castle.

It represents the elegance and strength of the castle. The towers also represent prosperous success in the Underworld. The scarlet color on the castle has a different meaning. The scarlet color on the castle means an evil individual is living there. Ruby gems were chosen for this castle because Verminia used rubies to show her opulence and evil.

There are also red diamonds, which are rare and illegal within this castle. The castle comprises of ten bedrooms. Nine of those bedrooms house the nine servants for the queen. Seven of those servants are males and two of them, females. Each servant's bedroom has one bathroom and a dresser. The beds in the servants' rooms are made of the traditional, obsolete feathers. Verminia has an opulent sleeping quarters.

Her sleeping quarters is forty feet by forty feet, the size of most suburban homes. She has a twenty feet in height crystal chandelier. The ceilings stand at fifty feet in height. The bed has transparent curtains. The curtains are made of a thin silk cloth. There's a dressing room in the bedroom. The mirror's frame is made of gold. The dressing room has different shelves. The shelves are made of silver and bronze. The floor is made of marble. The bathroom is extremely luxurious.

In spite of there not being any windows in the room, there's a bath, which has one hundred whirlpool jets. There's a walk-in towel closet and a hamper, which sends the laundry robotically to a washing machine. Then, the clothing is sent to a dryer and placed by a servant in the drawers, folded and pressed. There's a luxury ten by ten feet television, which is a 1080p television with high quality picture.

The sound on the television is very clear and eloquent. The room has speakers around the room. There are cameras within the room so Verminia basks in watching the servants constantly work. This is one of the ways to show she is tyrannical. She believes in arbitrary forced servitude. The queen is in her living area. The living area has one hundred feet in height ceilings. The living area has a comfortable couch.

This couch has ornate design patterns, which tell the story about the creation of the Underworld. The design patterns depict the Underworld as being a place that is one step before Hell. This is the place for the ones who caused themselves to end up in malevolent situations, which caused them to end up here.

The design depicts the souls, who've wronged others in their time alive, being sent to the Underworld. There's a massive footrest, which also serves as a purpose for a futon couch. The carpet in the center has a design of Skull Castle. There's a bust of Jacqueline.

There's an organ in the center of the castle. The doorbell is ringing. The noise of the doorbell sounds like the bells of Westminster Abbey. The stagecoach arrived at the castle. While Rubi was ringing the doorbell, William was thanking the driver. He did not give him any form of gratuity. The stagecoach departed. In spite of William being very parsimonious, the stagecoach driver showed kindness and compassion by giving a simple wave.

"Your majesty, there are guests at the front door, who want to meet you. I think you should answer the door", said the servant.

"No, why should I have to walk about fifteen feet to the door?" asked the queen.

"Because they are waiting for you and they are waiting to visit you. I think they are interested in speaking with you. I think they want to get to know you. The more constituents in existence supporting you, the better your evil agenda will be, your majesty", answered the servant.

"Wow. You actually know how to say,

'your majesty', at the first part of the sentence. How many times did I tell you to address me first as your majesty? I have probably told you about thirty million times. And don't take my words literally. I am just exaggerating the truth. However, I did tell you a large number of times this statement. Your behavior is uncalled for. The next time you do not address me as your majesty, I will have you punished and banished from this kingdom. If this is one of my bad days, I will have you executed. I mean it. Don't test my patience. Answer the damn door and escort the guests to me. Also, tell the other servants to make me a royalty dish. I feel hungry. Tell them to make me an antipasto dish", said the queen.

The servant escorted Rubi and William to the door. They bowed down to the queen.

"What are you doing here? Do you want some food?" asked Verminia.

"No, do you remember your sister, Jacqueline?" asked the alien leader's wife.

"Of course, I remember her. Your husband was the one who killed my sister and I want to get back at him. Sadly, I am stuck in this Underworld and I can't do a damn thing about it. I want to have him killed", answered the queen.

"Good, with me being here, we will get that done. First, I want to go down to the Secret Lair to have Jacqueline and the prisoners who were shot by the Ray Gun released", replied Rubi.

She is seeing a picture of a serpent. There's a flicker in the serpent's eye. The flicker looks like it was deliberately created by the artist. She is staring at the picture.

"Hold on a minute", she said.

She walked up to the picture and removed it from the wall. She slammed her fist against the blinking light. Consequently, smoke started leaving the light. Within thirty seconds, a loud, glass shatter has been heard. Rubi walked up to the explosion of glass and saw a flight of steps. She started running down the stairs. There, the fugitives are encapsulated in crystal freezers. They are frozen in time.

The following fugitives frozen in time are Jacqueline, Elitrionic, Mitchell, Howard, and Korbian.

"Should I release them?" asked the alien leader's wife.

"Let me come down there and see who they are. Then, I shall give you the approval or disapproval of releasing them", answered Verminia.

She ran down the stairs. William remained upstairs.

"Oh my God. My sister, she was down here. That damn Will. We shall go after him. We will kill him now. He imprisoned and frozen my sister. I bet you it was because he was much different than her. We will kill him. I hereby order you to release them", said Elitrionic. Rubi pulled the lever and released the sinister beasts. They all gasped for air.

"Elitrionic, what's your real name?" asked Rubi.

"I'll tell you later. My name is to remain confidential. I have to return to Starmos City to take the spot from the one who stole it from me. He must die", answered Elitrionic. He has left the castle.

"Jacqueline, I am so glad to see you. I miss you so much. What happened to you?" asked the queen.

"I belabored to make Starmos City a great place. I went as far as kidnapping Light to regain control of Starmos City; but of course, Will won the battle. Will wins everything. It is a shock. It is a disgrace that this city was taken over by him. Now, we must regain control. We will sentence the dissidents, the citizens of Starmos City to life in the hole without parole. We will ensure that they are tortured. We will win", the sinister former prosecutor said.

An evil laugh left both her mouth and

Verminia's mouth.

"Will, oh I remember that piece of garbage. He was the one that turned me on the evil side when I found out he was against Jacqueline's agenda. He had me placed in a cell and he wasn't really the full formal leader of the city. I need to get revenge back on him", said Howard.

"Will, that damn low life. He had me fired from the embassy and he made me look bad in front of my boss. He made me feel extremely angry. He was the one who destroyed my life. He left me with no other choice but to live on Swinburn Island. Now, he's the one who shall pay the price. Now, there'll be a second instance where I'll be left with no other choice but to kill him. Death shall do its part against him", said the sinister Mitchell.

"Will, that monstrosity; that piece of dung. He is nothing but excrement. He was the one who forced me down here. I was trying to fight for justice when I killed Gairdon. I was trying to seek revenge against him when I killed his beloved friend because he deserved that kind of revenge. Now, that I am back, I will have the opportunity to have my justice. He'd thought he had his justice; but now, I will have my justice. My justice will be killing him on the spot", said the evil Korbian.

"Now, that we are all here. We must cut

the chatter and start the splatter, that splatter being the gut spatter. Then, we must make his guts along with himself disappear. He was stupid enough to send you guys down here. We will make sure that we're not stupid enough to send him down here. We will make sure we send him in the air and that his vaporized remains are scattered all over the place so that way his body does not re-form and become Will again. We must kill him. He must be dead, dead, dead! So, I want every single one of you and I will join to run up the hills of the Underworld, cut through the jungle, catch up with Elitrionic, and run down the track because we're not going to have any proper transportation to Starmos City", declared Verminia.

"Aye", every villain said.

They ran out of the Scarlet Crystal Castle and started running through the hills of town. They pushed through all the ghosts, who have been present in the Fammer Alley and saw Elitrionic in front of the W. Ridley's Coffee Shop.

"What are we going to do from here?" asked Jacqueline. "We must raid the shop of all the coffee so we can receive unlimited energy", answered Elitrionic. W. Ridley III gave the sinister group of monstrosities the coffee. They are drinking the coffee at high speeds. After drinking the coffee, they started running towards the exit. They reached the doors. "Who goes here?" asked Leo.

"It is I, Jacqueline and my fellow brigade must enter", answered the demonic Langyaw.

"Wait. Don't let them in yet. I have to seek approval", said Leonard.

While the evil brigade wants to enter past the doors, Light and Wilheim are waiting at the train station.

"Go, you guys. Get out of here", the vivacious door knocker said to the LSC and the alien leader's cousin.

"Why?" asked Light.

"Because Jacqueline is coming after you. She's escaped. I am being serious. I know it sounds unbelievable; but it's the truth", Leonard answered frantically.

"I'll remain", replied the LSC.

"Then, you'll be screwd", replied the vivacious door knocker.

The evil brigade heard the conversation. Jacqueline is crazed.

"I demand you let us in! They're present. Perfect time to kill them", she screamed.

She started kicking the right door. She is jump kicking the door. A loud breaking of wood has been heard. She kicked the door once more. She smirked in a deceitful manner and growled. She is craving to kill Light and Wilheim like a Lion craving to kill a Zebra and Gazelle.

She is drooling with evil. She ran through the door.

"Run, Light! Get out of here", shouted Leonard.

Light shapeshifted into a train and Wilheim jumped on board immediately. Both escaped; and returned back to Starmos City. Wilheim jumped out of the LSC. Light shapeshifted back into a robot. They've eventually reached the estate. They ran through the secret chamber and to the library. The Blanco Brothers are hiding.

They are following Light and Wilheim up the stairs slowly. Light ran into the parlor room and reached Will, who is relaxing on the couch, viewing the front lawn. Light and Wilheim are panicking. The Blanco Brothers are in the kitchen.

"We must wait to kill him. We must hear the conversation first. We must find a way to make sure they are dead. We don't care if anybody knows they and Will die", said Miles.

"No, you don't understand. You are wrong. We must be covert in our operation. We must make sure that Will is dead. We should do some surveillance in the conversations. Then, we must strike. If you think we can wait for the military to come in, you're wrong. We must strike. And we must pull a surprise attack", replied Bill.

"No, you don't know what to do. Let's listen to the conversations. And then, we must shoot him. They know about our plan because Light and Wilheim are telling him about the plan", said the more practical brother (Miles.)

Meanwhile, the conversation between Light, Wilheim, and Will is taking place.

"Why are you breathing so heavily?" asked the alien leader.

"Because we were running from an evil militia. You won't believe this; but this is true. Jacqueline, Mitchell, Korbian, Elitrionic, Howard, Verminia, Rubi, and William Ridley jr. are coming after you. They are going to assasinate you. Additionally, the Blanco Brothers are out to get you. Officer Kerilic, I don't believe is here to kill you. He thought I was in association with Rubi. He fired a mass laser. You are not going to believe me; but would I lie to you about such a thing?" Wilheim asked nervously.

"No, but I am shocked that my own life would be so conniving in an evil plot to assasinate me", answered the alien leader.

"She only married you to use you. She doesn't believe in any deity. She supported Cornelius. She was acting pretentious to be on your side the whole time. She's against you, Will! She's here to harm you and destroy your life. She is a deleterious woman. She is nothing but a phony", said the alien leader's cousin.

Will is shocked.

"Fine. I will send down four hundred troops in the estate and have them appear in every room when these villains come after me", he said.

The Blanco Brothers entered the room. They are showing an evil glare towards Will.

"You are not going to get away with this", said Miles.

"Get away with what?" asked the alien leader.

"Get away with being the Leader of Starmos City unlawfully", answered the more practical brother.

"Excuse me, let me tell you something, you do not tell me that I was taking over the

President of Starmos City position unlawfully. Cornelius was running the city in a sinister manner. He was here to destroy the lives of the citizens. He was against the rights of the citizens. He committed crimes against humanity. He received his justifiable sentence. His confidants destroyed the lives of the citizens. His confidants were very deleterious. They brought more violence to the city more than he did. His confidants were extremely volatile, especially Jacqueline. I took over the leadership for a good reason. Maybe, in his eyes, it was unlawful. However, in my eyes, I was justified. In the citizens' eyes, they felt relieved that I took over. As for the presidential position, I became president by not abusing my power. Rather, I became the president by having an election and referendum and the large majority of the citizens supported me for the presidential position. For the ones who have opposed me, I have given them the floor to speak as long as they acted peaceful and professional, not volatile and sinister like you. Let me be clear to you, you are not going to assassinate me. I will have my guards go after you. I am not royalty but I am allowed to be protected from unjustifiable harm. You are an imminent threat to this city and imminent threats should learn to stay the hell away from me! #1, keep your mouth shut! You are acting unprofessional in terms of speaking your mind. You do have freedom of speech. You do have a voice in the government. You don't have freedom to kill, you maliciously brazen beast! #2, animalistic savages like yourself are not welcome into this city! So, get the hell out of this estate! If you think, for one second, I can't fight my own battles, you are wrong. I can fight! I am not weak! I just need help. If you can have an army, so can I", Will said boldly.

"You, shut the hell up! You are a hazard to Starmos City! I don't get this about you, Tyrant Will Von Alien. You claim that you let different folks open their mouths. Yet, you don't let people like myself have a voice in the government. How come that's the case? Are you afraid that my ideas are against yours? Is that what you are afraid of? Is my brazen attitude making you act in a craven manner? Is that the reason why you have a military behind you? Unlike you, I am not a coward. When you led the revolution against the government, you ran from the law. You did not challenge the law. Yet, you managed to become the Leader of Starmos City. I guess being craven is a good thing. I guess being a scaredy cat like you is good! May the evilness rain on your parade as leader. May your sinister attitude cause you to get life in the hole without parole like what happened to you. And the worst part was that you've betrayed Cornelius. You've betrayed your own cousin, which is nothing but a disgrace. You belong in a hole and you shall be buried six feet below the ground. Better yet, you shall disintegrate into the air. That's what shall happen to you, for you are a volatile and violent beast. You prey on the vulnerable like myself. You act like a jock. I don't like jocks. You think who the hell you are. You are nothing but a small leader. You do not show any leadership qualities because at that State Of The Union speech, all the words that were coming out of your mouth were nothing but rhetoric. You are nothing special to Starmos City. You are nothing of great importance to this place. You have not contributed a bit. You have just be rid this city of the good. You have derided the great ruler, Cornelius, and your murderous attitude has taken away his life. You are just like all those other dictators, who call themselves presidents", argued Mitchell. "Don't you dare call me a murderous tyrant because you are the one who supports the murderous tyrant. So, maybe, you should learn to shut your damn piehole. You are more of a danger to Starmos City than anybody is. The words that left my mouth were not rhetoric. There weren't any good values before my time. There weren't any morals before my time. The government was not good. The government was malevolent, beastly, ghastly, and evil. I was not like him because I did not imprison any of my dissidents. I only imprisoned those and executed those who wanted to assassinate me. And I sure as hell did not imprison the ones unjustly like Cornelius did. I did not have a five minute procedure and say 'GUILTY' without having a formal presentation of evidence in open court. I did make sure plea deals were offered. I did make sure that there would be a fair shot for the victims and the defendants. I made sure there was a double jeopardy clause in the Constitution of Starmos City. I did make sure that not any criminal would be arbitrarily punished. The criminals that have been prosecuted so far were the ones who've committed atrocities against the citizens, those atrocities being committed by Cornelius, Jacqueline, Serpianto, and Korbian. Keep that vile slander in your bloody mouth! You are a beast because you support the evil side", the alien leader said in a blunt manner.

"Give me the gun", Mitchell told his brother.

All of a sudden, ten guards emerged from the bushes and jumped through the glass of the parlor room. One thousand shards of glass are scattered across the floor.

"Drop the gun", said Officer Kerilic.

"No! I shall do no such thing", the practical brother replied bluntly.

Officer Kerilic reiterated what he'd just said. Mitchell did not drop the gun. He shot at the officers.

"Shoot the arsenic rifles", he commanded.

They shot needles of arsenic from the guns. Both brothers fell to the floor and died. The battle is not over yet. There are still militants ready to attack. The alien leader, the officers, Light, and Wilheim entered the hallway. One of the officers retrieved the gun from Mitchell.

"Open fire", screamed Rubi.

Jacqueline, Mitchell, Howard, Elitrionic, Rubi, William, and Verminia are in the hallway. They did not fire the guns.

"Remember me?" asked Jacqueline.

"What about me?" asked Elitrionic.

"Do you remember how you had me imprisoned?" asked Howard.

"And how you destroying my job?" asked Mitchell.

"Do you remember what you did to my sister?" asked Verminia.

"And how you helped destroy the Underworld?" asked William.

"Do you realize how stupid you are? I did not marry you to be the First Lady of Starmos City or to have Von Alien as my last name. I was really using you. I was really the one who was destroying your life. I married you to have you killed, frame it on one of your cabinet members, and bring back the old days of Cornelius. The stories I've told you about the boxcar life and escaping Russia were all false. My family was affluent. They've all just died off. I worked at the Star Hotel because I wanted to mooch off of them. Will, I am not good. I am evil and you are going down."

She retrieved a potion from her back pocket, beat him to the floor, and forced him to drink the quicksilver potion. Will gasped, his heart stopped, and immediately gave up in his journey of life.

"You murderer. I am going to have you executed for sure", screamed Light.

Four hundred guards stormed through the doors and windows of the estate, forced the perpetrators to drop their weapons, and apprehended them. The next day, the criminals were brought to trial. Protests outside the Starmos City courthouse are taking place. The citizens are protesting on behalf of Will and his family.

Banners stating, "Execute the Villians. We want Justice", are being shown.

The citizens are chanting, "Justice for Will Von, Justice for Will Von!" They are reiterating their chants for the entire length of the trial. The defendants represented themselves because not a single legal firm in Starmos City wanted to represent them and Light represented the prosecution. Opening arguments began in the morning and closing arguments began in the evening. The jury is about to deliver the verdict.

"For the Superior Court of Starmos City, as to the case against William Ridley Jr., we the jury find the defendant not guilty for aiding a fugitive. As to the case against Elitrionic, we the jury find the defendant guilty for posing as an alias name and capital murder. As to the case against Jacqueline Langyaw, we the jury find the defendant guilty of capital murder and unlawful burglary. As to the case against Rubi Worschinskiwitz Von Alien, we the jury find the defendant guilty of capital treason, capital murder, conspiracy to commit murder, and aiding fugitives on five counts, we the jury find the defendant guilty. We find that the defendant used a firearm to kill her own husband. As to the case against Mitchell, we the jury find the defendant guilty of capital murder. As to the case against Verminia Langyaw for capital murder, violating sovereignty for unjustifiable purposes, we the jury find the defendant guilty of those crimes", the jury has spoken. All jurors were polled and all agreed to the verdict. "The jury delivered the verdicts. W. Ridley, I adjudge you to be innocent, you are free to go. However, we will have you deported back to the Underworld. Jacqueline, Mitchell, Rubi, Elitrionic, and Verminia, I adjudge you to be guilty. Does the jury have the sentencing ready?" asked the judge.

"Yes, your honor", answered the juror.

"Wait. I am Cornelius Von Alien. I posed as Elitrionic to trick you. That's my alias name! I am still evil", said Elitrionic, who's really Cornelius.

The co-defendants smirked.

"I don't care if you're Cornelius or not. You are guilty of those charges the jury convicted you on and contempt of court. For contempt of court, you are sentenced to thirty days probation", said the judge.

He then asked the jury for the sentencing verdict.

"We find the factors of cruelty warrant the death penalty by arsenic injection, disembowelment, dismemberment, and the laser squad for all defendants. This is to make sure they don't come back from the dead ever", said the foreperson.

The defendants were sentenced to death and executed. Their body parts were scattered throughout the Starmos desert and dissintegrated. This is the beginning of a new Starmos City, where the tyranny is eradicated for once and all.

In spite of Will losing his life, a new president entered office, General Valencia is the new President of Starmos City.

He was elected in a Special Election with 70% of the vote. He maintains Will's cabinet and maintains Will's ideologies. Starmos City has expanded with the opening of new infastructures.

15 Years Later

Starmos City has expanded from once a city of a small skyline to a bustling city. The economy has tremendously increased. The travel has increased. The airport has been open and several autobahns expedite the journey into the city.

The autobahns lead the traveler from Earth, Garden City, Land of Noma, and Debonville into the city. WVA Boulevard will always maintain the same name. President Valencia has been elected 8 times. The population increased to one million. There are many new high density, medium density, and low density residences in the city. Many new small businesses opened up, and there'll long existing socialist ideology has been destroyed. Starmos City has changed for the better.

Epilogue

Freedom. Freedom is something that can unfortunately be attacked but never destroyed or eradicated. Freedom is something that shall always be cherished. It never is given from a silver platter. It is attained through hard work and leading crusades for justice. However, once a place attains freedom, it is hard for that to be destroyed. Freedom doesn't mean one can cause harm or be malevolent to others. Rather, freedom means that one can express himself or herself through peaceful speech, assembly, religion, and the nonlibel press. Freedom means justice, peace, kindness, and fairness. Freedom clearly does not mean damage, belligerence, and bellicose behavior. The ones who will try to eradicate, attack, or destroy freedom will never win and lose in the long run. Those who fight for freedom shall be lauded for their benevolent and sacrificial actions.

About The Author: Joseph Salvatore Pidoriano

Joseph Salvatore Pidoriano is a seventeen year old man from Staten Island New York. He currently attends Xaverian High School in Brooklyn, New York. He is planning on opening up two theme park resorts in New York and New Jersey, as of March 2015. He has written the Dimension Travel Books to bring success for his future company's

development. He is also planning on running for political office under the Republican Party (Independence, Women's Equality Party, and StopCommonCore Party, as supporter parties.)

www.ingramcontent.com/pod-product-compliance
Lightning Source LLC
Chambersburg PA
CBHW071307200626
46813CB00015B/492